ALIAS™

DISAPPEARED

Alias: Disappeared

A Bantam Book / March 2003
Text and cover art copyright © 2003 by Touchstone Television

ISBN: 0-553-49400-7

Visit us on the Web! www.randomhouse.com

Published simultaneously in the United States and Canada

Bantam Books is an imprint of Random House Children's Books, a
division of Random House, Inc. BANTAM BOOKS and the rooster
colophon are registered trademarks of Random House, Inc. Bantam
Books, New York.

PRINTED IN THE UNITED STATES OF AMERICA

OPM 10 9 8 7 6 5 4 3 2 1

ALIAS™

DISAPPEARED

Lynn Mason

AN ORIGINAL PREQUEL NOVEL BASED ON THE
HIT TV SERIES CREATED BY J. J. ABRAMS

BANTAM BOOKS
NEW YORK ★ TORONTO ★ LONDON ★ SYDNEY ★ AUCKLAND

1

THE PAPER AIRPLANE SOARED *upward, grazing the bottom branches of the sycamore tree before skidding to a stop on the grass. Sydney raced across the yard to retrieve it, the plaid pleated skirt of her girls' academy uniform swirling about her long, thin legs.*

"Daddy! Daddy, look! I made it fly!"

Mr. Bristow's head remained hidden behind the front section of the Los Angeles Register.

"Daddy?" Sydney asked, taking a few steps toward him. "Daddy, you aren't listening to me. I made a good plane! It flew really far! Didn't you see?"

"Yes. I saw," came a flat response.

"No! You didn't!" she yelled, stamping her burgundy penny loafer. *"You weren't watching, you were reading! That's all you do all the time! Read, read, read!"*

The paper lowered and Mr. Bristow's blank expression fell on his daughter. "Stop being dramatic, Sydney," he said. "You're acting like a child."

But I *am* a child, *she thought, angrily tossing the plane into the air again. It sailed straight up for a few seconds before becoming wedged in a tangle of twigs. She turned back toward her father, hoping he would offer to pull it loose. But his newspaper barrier was raised once again, and all Sydney could see were the large black letters screaming* SPACE SHUTTLE EXPLODES!

*　*　*

"Hey? You awake?" Todd de Rossi's voice penetrated the daydream.

Sydney jerked her head slightly. "Huh? What?" The childhood memory dissolved as she found herself back in her American History seminar, her pen still poised over her spiral notebook. Professor Baldridge was lecturing in his tired drone, his words melding with the steady whir of the old building's air-conditioning system. On the giant screen behind him loomed the famous image of the *Challenger* exploding high in the atmosphere.

"Sorry," she whispered, smiling weakly at Todd. "What did you say?"

Todd grinned. "I said it takes a special kind of boring to make a major disaster dull. Guess I made my case. Where were you just now? In orbit?"

"No. I was just . . . I was just remembering where I was when I first heard about the *Challenger* exploding." She rubbed her eyes and sat up straight, trying to shake off the residual anguish stirred up by her memory. She could practically smell the olive trees shading the Bristows' old front porch and feel the light weave of her school uniform, as if her body had carefully recorded every sensation for careful replay later on.

It had been one of those pivotal childhood moments: the point when she'd finally understood that her father was lost to her. The tragic car accident that had taken her mother seemed to have completely diminished her father. He had never been the cheerful life force her mother was, and yet Sydney had never doubted his devotion to his family. But that day on the front lawn, all hope that he might someday come back to her shattered like the hull of the ill-fated space shuttle. From then on she stopped consciously trying to please him and began preparing herself for a life alone.

"You know, I don't remember what I was doing

when I first heard about the *Challenger,*" Todd mused, rubbing his chin. "Probably standing in front of my mirror doing my best James Dean."

Sydney rolled her eyes. "Why does that not surprise me?"

"Excuse me? Professor Baldridge?" Sydney glanced up to see a tall guy with shaggy red hair rise from his aisle seat, his left arm high in the air.

"Oh, goody. Burke has something to say," Todd whispered, leaning forward in his seat. "This ought to be entertaining."

Most of the other students in the lecture hall were also shifting to get a better look. Sydney let out a small moan of frustration and slouched back in her chair, folding her arms across her striped sweater. Great. Another outburst from Burke Wells, campus radical extraordinaire.

Professor Baldridge's reaction was not unlike her own. "Yes, Mr. Wells?" he asked, his voice sounding more weary than usual.

"Isn't it true, Professor," Burke began, "that the shuttle blew up due to sabotage and not because of an accident?"

The professor heaved a long, audible sigh. "No, Mr. Wells. I'm afraid that was simply a story a few tabloids used to try to sell papers. As I said earlier, the explosion was caused by a faulty—"

"Excuse me, Professor," Burke interrupted, waving his arm in the air again. "But it wasn't just in the tabloids, was it? I mean, sure, it wasn't reported in any of the so-called legitimate, corporate-run U.S. papers. But several highly esteemed foreign news agencies reported the existence of a top-secret surveillance satellite aboard, which was the motive behind the sabotage."

Sydney shook her head in disbelief. "What's *up* with this guy?" she grumbled.

"Don't know. Isn't he dreamy, though?" Todd's large brown eyes seemed to droop as they beheld Burke. Sydney glanced around the room. Dozens of girls were staring at Burke with the exact same puppy dog expression.

"Full of himself is more like it," she said.

"No, Burke's cool," Todd countered. "I've gone to a couple of demonstrations he's organized. The guy knows a lot about human rights violations and government cover-ups. He feels it's his duty to tell people the truth about stuff. Things they don't tell you in college."

Sydney squinted at Burke. His knit cap and woven Guatemalan shirt were standard-issue hippie radical, although he wore athletic shoes. His arms were lean and well toned, thanks to a regimen of one-hour yoga sessions, a strict vegetarian diet, and lots of dancing to bongos, she guessed. Of course, the most in-your-face thing about Burke Wells was how beautiful he was. His scruffy appearance implied the absence of massive vanity, but it was hard to hide the Green party's version of Brad Pitt.

That was just it. He was almost *too* handsome. His features were oh-so-perfectly proportioned and symmetrical, his eyes were fairy-tale bright and twinkly, and those thick red waves that grazed the tops of his broad shoulders looked as if they belonged in a shampoo ad. Never mind his ad-libbed approach to history. Sydney always had trouble trusting anyone that perfect-looking.

"I don't buy it. Most of what he says in class sounds like nonsense," she muttered. "He probably just likes attention."

Todd shook his head. "I don't think so. Guys who look like Burke don't have to work to make people notice them."

Sydney frowned. Todd had a point there. But come on! A spy satellite on a space shuttle? That was delusional. Plus, it made the government—the same government she was trained to risk her life for—sound idiotic and devious.

Having made his point, Burke once again took his seat, and Professor Baldridge continued his speech. Students all around them slouched back in their chairs.

"You know," Todd whispered, leaning toward

her, "I think you and Burke would really hit it off. Want me to introduce you?"

"No." Todd was sweet, but all those Diet Cokes he drank must have reached toxic levels in his blood.

"Aw, come on."

"No!" She'd been insulted by arrogant pretty boys like Burke before, and she was not going through it again. "I'm serious, Todd. No setups, okay? Promise me you won't introduce me to that guy."

Todd crossed his hand over his heart and held up his first three fingers. "Scout's honor," he said, staring back with his big, soulful eyes. "You can count on me."

* * *

"Burke!" Todd called as they made their way out into the hall after class.

In the sea of moving faces, Burke's red hair stuck out like a campfire in the crowd. He looked over at them and smiled. "Hey, Todd. What's going on?" he said, altering his path to head toward them.

Sydney clamped her hand tightly on Todd's arm. "Didn't you promise me you wouldn't do this?" she muttered through her teeth.

"Sorry, Sydney," he replied with an impish grin. "I was never a scout."

Burke shuffled up to them, still smiling. Sydney

was amazed—dismayed, actually, to see he was even better-looking close up. From this distance she could see the faint cleft in his chin. And his almond-shaped hazel eyes held so many colors, she wondered if they'd been tie-dyed.

But in her experience, the better-looking a guy was on the outside, the more of a jerk he was inside. She just might have to kill Todd for his good intentions.

"Hey, that was some great stuff you brought up in class," Todd said. "Really got me thinking."

Without meaning to, Sydney let a slight snort escape through her nostrils. Burke raised his eyebrows.

"Um . . . this is my friend Sydney." Todd said, jabbing her with his elbow. "She's sort of . . . a skeptic."

"Hi, I'm Burke," he greeted her, offering his hand. She took it, grudgingly, and gave it a shake. "So what are you skeptical about?"

Sydney pulled back her hand, opened her mouth to say something, and then quickly shut it. Even disregarding Todd's elbow drilling into her rib cage, she really wasn't sure she wanted to get into this. But if she dodged the question, she'd only end up looking cowardly. And she hated to let this guy get away with all his misguided propaganda.

"This whole business about the satellite," she began. "It's ludicrous. Everyone knows NASA uses unmanned rockets to launch things like that. Besides, the *Challenger* mission was all about education and good PR for the space program. Why would they allow a spy satellite on board?"

Burke nodded along with her. "You're right. But see, that's precisely *why* officials wanted to use the mission. Because no one would suspect it."

She shook her head. "That still makes no sense. Suppose they *did* have top-secret spy equipment on board. The launch was being closely covered by the media. How could anyone get close enough to sabotage it?"

"Good point," Burke replied. Sydney searched his voice for any hidden condescension but found none. "Still," he added, "you have no idea what some of these anti-American groups are capable of."

A bemused expression flitted across her face. *Just try me, pal,* she muttered silently. *I've seen stuff that would straighten your hair.*

"From what I understand," he went on, "they did manage to penetrate security, probably with inside help. And the media coverage only worked in their favor. They were able to humiliate U.S. officials and send them a loud, obvious message about their spy operations."

Sydney sighed. She really wished he would wipe that smile off his face. It was just so absurdly warm and friendly and charming, it was completely defusing her aggravation. "Look. You seem like a nice guy," she said in a tone she typically reserved for children or the mentally imbalanced. "But I've got to say, someone's been feeding you a lot of bogus information."

"Maybe," he said with a shrug. "But have you ever stopped to question the information you've been getting?"

Sydney blinked at him. If he only knew what she did for a living. For his own security!

"Well, I gotta go." Burke stepped around them and continued down the corridor. "Bye, Todd," he called over his shoulder. "Nice to meet you, Sydney."

"Man oh man," Todd murmured as he watched him walk away. "I'm real sorry, Sydney."

"That's okay," she replied. "I know you meant well."

"No. I don't mean that. I mean about thinking you two would hit it off," Todd explained. "Boy, was I ever wrong."

"I told you," she said, shoving his shoulder.

"But if Burke isn't your type, who the hell is?"

Sydney shrugged. She couldn't tell Todd about another pivotal moment in her life . . . the moment she had first laid eyes on Noah Hicks.

2

SYDNEY PULLED HER WHITE Mustang into her
usual space in the SD-6 parking garage, turned off the
engine, and angled the rearview mirror toward her.
Her long chestnut hair tumbled about her shoulders in
subtle waves. Lip-gloss shone on her plump lips. And
her deep-set brown eyes glittered with anticipation—
even if they did dart around nervously a bit. She was
as ready as she'd ever be. Ready to see *him*.

It had been four days since their parting at the
Paris airport, and she hadn't been able to stop thinking about Noah Hicks: his rough-hewn good looks,
his rumbly voice, and that walk—equal parts prowl

and glide. She even found his name irresistible. Noah. No-*ahhh*. Like a long, contented sigh.

She'd been desperately trying to recategorize these feelings, telling herself that Noah was a coworker—a superior, in fact. Totally off limits. But no mental Post-its could stem the warm, quivery sensations that flooded her whenever he entered her thoughts, which lately was all the time.

A little teleplay of how their next meeting would proceed had already been written in her mind. She would say something witty. He would laugh that sexy, growly laugh of his. Their gazes would lock and an unspoken communiqué would pass between them, a silent promise they could hold on to until they could hold each other again. Music would swell. Young girls would weep into their popcorn. People everywhere would clutch their chests and sigh. . . .

Or at least, that's what she *hoped* would happen.

Their time in Paris, while not exactly romantic, had been full of potential. And the mission had been a complete success. She and Noah had managed to completely dismantle a K-Directorate money-laundering operation, using a plan she devised herself. The experience helped her feel capable as an agent, and it felt good to know she'd thwarted some of her country's enemies. But highlighting it all was the closeness she had developed with Noah. They really seemed to bond as friends and comrades in battle, if nothing else. But, of course, there had also been that kiss. . . .

She'd replayed the scene a thousand times. Their frantic embrace in the dark alcove, their bodies still wet and slippery from their swim through the Seine. His mouth searching hers, her hands exploring his muscular chest . . .

It had only been a cover to throw off the stranger that had surprised them, in case he'd been an enemy agent. But it had felt *real*.

Sydney had never experienced such emotions. Oh, she'd had crushes before—horrible, silly infatuations with guys who'd ended up being nothing like she imagined. But with Noah it was something more real. Deeper. Crazier. Scarier. The hardest thing was, she had no idea how he felt about her. There were times—a long gaze, a mysterious grin—when she seemed to pick up a definite vibe. And then there were times when she was certain it was all wishful thinking. Not that it mattered. The main thing was that they'd really connected. You can't risk your life with someone and not become intimate.

"Okay, Syd." She took a deep breath and nodded at her reflection. "Get a grip." She grabbed her leather attaché, leaped from the car, and went up the stairwell to the bank's ground floor, her suppressed nervousness powering her long legs at a furious pace. After spending most of the week taking care of some final details in Europe, Noah had flown back early this morning. In a few minutes she'd be face to face with him at their debriefing with Wilson.

As soon as she stepped into the lobby, she saw Noah standing in front of the elevators. A buzz of electricity surged through her, accelerating her breath and heartbeat. For a moment she stood rooted to the polished marble floor. Even in his freshly pressed suit he stood out from the rest of the neatly dressed business types scurrying through the foyer. For one thing, he was the only one not wearing a tie. But beyond that, there was always something innately rough and unkempt about Noah Hicks that no Armani suit could hide. She loved that about him.

The elevator doors opened, and Noah turned and loped into the shiny metal lift. Sydney suddenly snapped to attention. "Noah!" she shouted, her voice echoing through the vast lobby. People stared. Noah craned his neck, searching the room. She raised her hand and ran forward. "Hey, Noah! Wait up!"

As she hurried toward the elevator, she thought she perceived a small grin wash across his face. His uneven features softened slightly and then reset themselves. A second later she entered the elevator, and the doors slid shut behind her.

"Hey," she said, gasping for breath. "You're

back." *Duh, Syd*, she thought, wincing inwardly. Not exactly the smart opening she'd been hoping for.

Noah gave a brisk nod and stared up at the number panel. "I got in this morning. Wilson wants my final report on our mission," he added, tapping his black leather briefcase.

Sydney's lips curved automatically at his use of the phrase "our mission." That's exactly what it had been. Theirs. Just the two of them, united in the face of danger.

"Yeah, what a mission," she began, shaking her head. "It was amazing. Really awesome." *Awesome?* Wasn't that the type of thing a preteen with glitter nail polish would say? Noah was over seven years older than she was. No reason to call further attention to that minor detail.

She glanced over at him and studied his profile. Judging by the extra lift above his cheekbone, he seemed to be smiling. Or was it a grimace?

The subbasement floors lit up one after the other as the elevator continued to descend. Sydney felt a rush of panic. The ride seemed much too short. She wanted time to pick things up where they'd left them in Paris, to recapture that chummy intimacy that brewed between them.

She wished he would say something. Flash her one of those impish smiles and start up some playful banter.

Instead, he just stood there, one hand stuffed in the pocket of his trousers, casually rocking in his loafers.

The doors opened and they stepped into the white scanning cubicle. Sydney couldn't take it anymore. As they stood on the large black circle, letting the red sensor light wash over them, she leaned toward him and laid a hand on his elbow. "Um, hey," she said with a hopeful grin. "I'm really glad you're back, Noah."

He turned and looked at her just as the front wall of the cubicle opened, revealing the noise and bustle of headquarters. "I am too," he murmured, his eyes staring right into hers. Sydney smiled. The flutters she'd felt in Paris returned at maximum strength. "But could you do something for me?" he asked, his voice low and serious.

"Sure," she breathed in reply.

"You should probably call me Agent Hicks," he said, and then calmly stepped out into the corridor.

Sydney couldn't move. *Agent Hicks?* But that was so impersonal. In Paris he'd been Noah. Didn't their near-death experience together mean anything?

She forced her limbs to propel her out of the scanning chamber and down the hall after Noah. Agent Hicks. Whoever he was. He certainly didn't seem like the same guy she'd hit it off with in Paris.

Don't freak out. It's no big deal, she told herself. But the more she tried to push it from her mind, the more she ended up obsessing. What exactly had he meant? That she was being too forward? Amateurish? Either way, it *was* a big deal.

They entered the op-tech room and sat down. Sydney was trying hard not to look at Noah, focusing instead on the newswire reports that were scrolling across the computer screen in front of her. It was just the default setting for the monitors, but Sydney would rather pretend to be riveted to the details of a train derailment in Germany than let Noah see how much he had hurt her. Screw it. If he wanted to be in work mode, fine. She'd be all current-events research and no small talk.

She could feel his eyes on her. He even coughed and shifted in his seat a couple of times as if he was going to say something but then changed his mind. Still she wouldn't look up.

To think she'd been fantasizing for days about seeing him again. She'd figured if anything, things could ease up more between them now that the mission was over. She'd envisioned them joking around in the corridors and reliving some of the most harrowing moments of the mission. She'd even had hopes of them meeting after work for coffee or dinner, where they could open up about their lives and really get to know one another.

She had not counted on Noah going all protocol on her.

Noah cleared his throat. "I wonder what's taking so long."

Sydney made herself look at him. He sat slouched in his chair, left ankle on right knee, lazily rapping his pen against the side of the conference table. As usual, his rocky features were impossible to read.

"Wilson's really making us wait today, huh?" he added, slowly twisting his chair back and forth.

"Mmm. Yeah," she replied, raising her eyebrows. "Really unprofessional of him, don't you think?"

She had a split second to savor the bewildered expression on Noah's face before the door flew open and Wilson lumbered into the room. "Hicks, Bristow," he said, nodding at each of them. "I've just read your report," he added, gesturing toward Noah with a stapled document in his right hand. "Excellent work. Both of you."

"Thanks," Sydney replied. Noah nodded, his eyes darting over to Sydney before focusing back on Wilson.

"I know we'd planned for an official debriefing today, but something has just come up." Wilson sat down at the head of the table and hit a button on the control panel in front of him. The photo of a woman in her mid twenties appeared on each of the room's computer screens.

"This photo was taken today," Wilson said. Sydney

thought the woman looked incredibly cold and angry for someone so young. Her short dark hair emphasized the stiff, angular lines of her face. Her eyes were hard and narrowed. And small fissures crept from the sides of her nose to the corners of her full-lipped mouth, giving the look of a permanent scowl.

"Adriana Lizuca Nichita," Wilson explained. "Heiress of the former ruling Nichita family of Romania. She's been living in exile since she was an adolescent. No longer welcome in her country, Nichita has nonetheless been clinging to power in Europe by using her vast fortune in hidden bank accounts to help finance clandestine deals in arms, drugs, and military and industrial intelligence. Yesterday, SD-6 sources managed to intercept a communication to her. However, Adriana Nichita has been in secret CIA custody for two days, charged with trying to bribe a high-ranking U.S. intelligence officer, so she never received the message."

"What did the communication contain?" Noah asked, frowning at his monitor.

Wilson hit a switch. Instantly a map of Europe materialized on the screens, zooming in on a tiny, landlocked country on the Balkan Peninsula. "What do you know about the nation of Suratia?" he asked.

Noah sat up straight, peering at Wilson with new interest. "An ancient principality that has had the same ruling family since the sixteenth century. Since it's unable to compete with the larger countries in the European market, Suratia has become famous as a hotbed of illegal activity. For over a century it has had a policy of averting its eyes while black marketers, arms merchants, mobsters, and black-op spies do their dealings. Any fugitive can find safe haven inside its borders. In exchange, these underworld organizations pay quarterly sums of money, arms, or other goods and follow a strict hands-off policy on Suratia's people and property." He looked right at Wilson, his bushy brows raising to perfect arches. "Why? How are they involved?"

Wilson grasped his chin between his thumb and forefinger. "Last week a private plane belonging to the ruling monarch, Prince Xavier, crashed after takeoff. Prince Xavier lies in a coma and is not expected to survive. The heir to the throne, his oldest son, Kristophe, was killed. Next in line to succeed him is his second son, Prince Frederique. Not much is known about Frederique except that he has always been passionate about putting an end to this back-door corruption. He is young and popular, especially with Suratia's military force, which, although small, is very nicely equipped. Obviously, the European underworld is in a panic."

He pressed the control button once again, and a photo of a steely-eyed man with a meticulously combed mustache appeared before them. "Herbert von Muller," Wilson went on. "His black market would seriously suffer from Suratia's policy change. To deal with the situation, he has scheduled a summit meeting between underworld representatives at one of his estates—the remote Balfour Manor off the western coast of Scotland. The message to Nichita contained an invitation to this meeting, which will be held two weeks from now. Sloane sees this as a tremendous opportunity to gain vital information on our European-based enemies. It is expected that a rep from K-Directorate's European cell will be there, as well as a member of Mercado de Sangre and other drug runners and arms dealers."

"Great," Noah said, nodding briskly. "So what's the plan?"

Wilson raised his hands and pressed his fingertips together. Then he exhaled sharply. "SD-6 wants Sydney to go to the summit," he said. "Alone."

"What?" The word burst out of Sydney's mouth before she could compose herself. For a moment, she forgot all about being angry with Noah. She looked over at him and saw that he too was gazing slack-jawed at Wilson.

"Adriana has rarely been photographed. With a little makeup artistry, Sydney could have a physical resemblance to her. Because of her linguistic aptitude,

Sydney could attend the meeting in Adriana's place and do valuable reconnaissance," Wilson went on. "We may never have such an opportunity again."

Sydney tried to unravel the tangle of emotions inside her. She was amazed and flattered that they would trust her with such an important job. But she was scared, too. What if she wasn't up to the task? After all, she'd only been on two real missions so far—one and a half, actually, since the first was thrust on her with no real preparation and without her knowing. Still, they wouldn't even consider her for this if they didn't think her capable . . . right?

Noah leaned forward and placed his hands on the tabletop. "What did you mean about her having to go in alone?"

Yeah, Sydney wondered. *What exactly* did *that mean?*

Wilson let out a long sigh. "Von Muller is an eccentric paranoid," he began. "He has insisted that no weapons or bodyguards be allowed during the meeting, for himself as well as the others. All parties will be searched for hidden tools and high-tech circuitry. Sydney will not be able to wear a com link. Balfour has no electricity. No telephone wires. We might be able to send messages to Sydney, but she will have no way of communicating with us. If she ends up exposed, or if the mission is compromised in any way, we won't be able to help her."

Sydney sat in stunned silence. Out of the corner of her eye, she could see Noah glance from her to Wilson and back again. She kept her gaze fixed on the map in front of her, letting Wilson's words ricochet through her mind. *Completely on my own . . . No help at all . . .* No Noah or Wilson to give advice or cover her back. No reassuring words mumbled through a hidden earpiece. And even though the thought of using a gun on someone still made her queasy, the thought of not having one strapped to her for protection was even more unsettling.

But still . . . they trusted her. They needed her. They were counting on her and her alone. Sydney turned these thoughts over and over in her mind like a lucky coin. In a way, she'd never felt so proud in her life.

"Sydney?" Wilson sounded as if he were calling from a faraway cliff.

She jerked herself out of her trance and looked up. "Yes?"

His gaze intensified. "I need to know before we go any further," he said, his gray-streaked brows scrolling together. "Knowing all these risks, are you willing to take on the mission?"

Yes. The word formed in her mind free of any real consideration. Of course she would go. No question.

Before she could answer aloud, Noah lifted his hand. "Wait a minute, wait a minute," he said, raising his other hand in Sydney's direction like a frantic traffic cop. "I don't think this is a good idea."

Sydney gaped at him. "Why not?"

"Yes, Agent Hicks," Wilson said, peering closely at Noah. "I'd like to hear your reasons for that opinion."

Noah drew back his arms and glanced over at Sydney. She got the distinct impression there was a silent message in his expressionless stare. What it was, though, she had no idea.

It was irritating as hell. For all her so-called genius with languages, she always felt like a complete imbecile when it came to reading Noah Hicks. And today he was particularly incomprehensible.

"As the leader of the Paris mission, I got to observe Bristow in the field," Noah began. "And I have to say . . . I don't think she's ready to take on an operation like this by herself."

Sydney crumpled forward slightly. How could he say that? She'd been good on the mission—*damn* good, in fact. He'd told her so himself! So why was he betraying her? Why was everything suddenly so different between them?

Wilson also seemed surprised by Noah's remarks. "This is very unexpected, Agent Hicks. Especially since your mission report contains nothing but high praise for Bristow's work." He patted the document on the table before him.

Sydney felt a bubble of hope. So she hadn't imagined things. He really had commended her. She looked back at Noah. His features remained stoic and cement-like, but there was an almost imperceptible change in his stance. A minuscule droop in his shoulders, an accelerated blinking of his eyelids.

"I'm not saying that Bristow isn't skilled, or that she doesn't have the potential to be a first-class agent," he said smoothly. "But she still lacks the necessary discipline and often reacts without thinking, tendencies that could easily spell disaster in a situation like this."

Once again Sydney felt a ripping sensation inside her. Her throat tightened and warm tears bathed her eyes, blurring Noah's face. She wanted to yell, but her breathing was too weak and ragged. She could only glare toward the hazy, distorted image of Noah swimming in front of her and crunch her thumbs inside her fists.

"I see," Wilson said.

Sydney glanced toward the blur that was Wilson, afraid of what he might say. Was this the end of her career at SD-6? Could this sort of negative feedback drum her out of the agency forever?

"Of course you have every right to voice your

opinion, Agent Hicks," Wilson said matter-of-factly. "However, SD-6 feels differently. The final decision is Sydney's," he said, pivoting in her direction. "Are you willing to go on this mission?"

Sydney's vision cleared. She took a deep breath and stared over at Noah. "Yes," she replied in a loud, determined voice. "You can count on me." *I'll show you,* she thought, keeping her eyes on Noah. *I'll show everyone I can handle this. Even myself.*

"Good," Wilson said. He pushed back his chair and stood, signaling the end of the meeting. "You'll begin intensive training immediately. In one week we will meet for a final briefing before your trip to Scotland."

Sydney rose from her chair. "Sounds good," she said, smiling. "Thanks, Wilson."

She turned to flash Noah one more look of triumph, but he wasn't in his seat. The door was open and he was already stalking down the crowded, narrow corridor.

I'M THE **BAD GUY** NOW.

BUT IT'S FOR HER OWN GOOD.

I HATED IT, THOUGH. THAT BRITTLE LOOK IN HER EYES. THAT CREASE THAT APPEARS DOWN THE MIDDLE OF HER FOREHEAD . . .

IT JUST ABOUT **KILLED** ME.

AND I LOST ANYWAY.

3

SYDNEY REMAINED STIFF AS a statue, concentrating with all her mental energy. Just a couple more seconds . . .

The pen teetered to the left. Sydney quickly compensated by tilting her head to the right a few millimeters, and the pen once again stabilized, its tip bouncing in the lower quadrant of her vision.

It hadn't been easy figuring out how to balance a pen on her nose, but she'd done it. The long, straight slope had had her at a disadvantage from the start. But luckily, she found that the small notch at the tip served as the perfect fulcrum if she raised her chin an inch or two.

She remained motionless in her chair, slightly cross-eyed as she fixed on the swaying fine-tipped Bic. It had probably been five whole minutes now. Maybe more . . .

"What the *hell* am I doing?" she exclaimed suddenly. She shook her head and the pen dropped to the floor, rolling under her writing desk.

Okay, so she was nuts. But hey, it wasn't like she had lots of really important things to do. Like study for her history exam. Or finish her essay on Chaucer. Or bone up on her Romanian for the top-secret, life-threatening spy mission she was going on in a week.

It was all Noah's fault. Damn him. She had tried to study her Romanian. For a while, it had been going along really well. The problem was that it was a lot like French. Which reminded her of Paris. Which reminded her of their mission. Which reminded her of what an utter creep he had been toward her the day before.

The familiar pangs returned. She was used to this sort of hurt happening within her desolated family life. Or her nearly extinct love life. *Not* SD-6. For several months it had been the one player in her life (besides Francie) that was completely loyal and committed to her. And now Noah had to louse that up. Now she had all kinds of negative feelings attached to her work. It was unfair. Even worse, it was dangerous.

I've got to get a grip, she told herself. *So I obvi-*

ously overestimated his feelings for me. So what. I can be big about this. I can be professional.

The way she figured it, Noah was either:

a) a traitorous scumbag who had only pretended to care about her during their mission in the interest of international policy, but who actually couldn't wait to get back to HQ and slander her name, or

b) telling the truth. Maybe he honestly thought she wasn't up to it. Maybe it wasn't enough that she'd covered his ass and come up with a plan that saved their entire mission.

She didn't like either option. Plus, neither one made sense. How could he be so convinced she wasn't ready for this job? Wilson and the top brass thought she was capable enough. And although she hadn't read his report, Noah had apparently commended her fieldwork in Paris. Her knowledge of the opposite sex might be preschoolish at best, yet she was savvy enough to know that he didn't hate her. She didn't know exactly what had been between them in Paris. Camaraderie? Flirtation?

It definitely hadn't been hatred.

She hunched back over her desk and reopened her history text. Inside lay a tall, thick, saddle-stitched paperback full of the Romanian words and phrases she'd been reviewing with the help of tapes at SD-6. She should at least study some good choice names she could call him. She had to hold on to this anger to keep from curling up on her bed and sobbing.

Hmmm. How would one say *jerk-off traitor* in Romanian?

At that moment, the door to her dorm room was flung open and Francie bounced in, all glittering eyes and high-wattage smile. She took one look at Sydney sitting at the desk and froze. Her eyebrows raised and the corners of her mouth drooped slightly.

"Uh . . . Syd? What are you doing?" she asked through her grin.

Sydney's eyes darted back and forth, searching for an audience or hidden camera. "I'm studying?" she replied slowly, sensing that it was the wrong answer.

"Syd!" Francie whined, her face falling completely. "I thought you'd be getting ready by now."

Sydney continued to look at her blankly. "For what?" she asked hesitantly.

Francie blinked at her, her features smoothing into a flat, frustrated stare. "Don't tell me you forgot," she mumbled.

Ohh-kay . . . I won't, Sydney thought. She flashed Francie a helpless look and gave a small shrug.

"The mixer!" Francie said, stepping forward and throwing up her arms in exasperation. "You promised you'd go with me!"

Oh, yeah. Now she remembered. Francie had

been so excited to hear about the party at . . . some frat. Sigma Delta Fee-Fie-Fo-Fum something. And since Francie was between worthy guys at the moment, Sydney had promised to go with her. But that had been before her mission assignment. Before Noah—damn him—had completely thrown her powers of concentration out of whack.

"I don't know, Fran," she began, gesturing toward the pile of books in front of her. "You see, I've got all this—"

"Reading. I know," Francie finished for her, her tone low and weary. "Jeez, Syd. Why not give yourself a break?" She plopped down on the edge of her bed and kicked off her red leather slides. "I don't mean to nag you. It's just that . . . well, all you ever do is read."

Her tone jarred something loose in Sydney's mind. Suddenly she heard her own voice, only smaller and more whiny. *That's all you do all the time! Read, read, read!*

Was she that bad?

Sydney sighed. Maybe she could go for a little while? Thanks to work, she hadn't been available to hang out with Francie much these past couple of weeks. She'd missed her. And if she kept begging off these nights of fun, it might end up jeopardizing their friendship.

"You know . . . you're right," Sydney said, reaching

out her leg and jostling Francie's bare foot with her sneaker. "What do you say we put on some to-die-for dresses and head out?"

Francie's smile returned. "You mean it?"

"Yeah."

She could do with a breather. After all, she wasn't exactly getting much done. Besides, it could end up being an excellent way to get her mind off everything. And every*one*.

* * *

"Isn't this great?" Francie cast her smile about the large, jam-packed frat-house living room.

"Yeah." Sydney glanced down at herself. She certainly looked as if she belonged. Her raspberry-colored halter dress and strappy sandals were definite standard-issue party wear. And she'd done up her hair in a funky retro ponytail. Beside her, Francie looked amazing in her white scoop tee, burgundy skirt, and the cutest, tiniest side-slung black purse that could barely hold her driver's license.

The problem was, Sydney had just never been a party gal. To some people (most, she'd venture to guess), a party was the ultimate in fun. To her, it was fun times eight hundred and sixty-three. Too much noise, too many strangers. It was stimulation to the point of agitation.

So she was a freak. She'd heard it all through boarding school. The teachers had called her a loner. The counselor had called her shy and reserved. Kids had called her a bookworm. But she could suck it up for one night, couldn't she? For the sake of Francie and their friendship?

"Oh. My. God! There he is!" Francie suddenly wrenched Sydney's arm and squeezed it tight.

"Who?"

"That guy."

Sydney followed Francie's eyes. All she could see were guys. "Who?" she asked again.

"You know. *That* guy. The one I've been talking about. From my logic class?"

"Ah yes. Logical Guy." For weeks Francie had been swooning over some hottie that she swore could be a lost Wayans brother. "Where is he?"

"Standing by the fireplace in the Forty-Niners sweatshirt. I think his name is Tyler, but I'm not sure."

Sydney looked. Sure enough, a tall, smooth-skinned hunk was leaning against the mantle, laughing along with a couple of his buddies. He had an amazing smile, just like Francie. So gleaming white, she couldn't make out individual teeth—like a cartoon-character grin.

"Isn't he gorgeous?" Francie asked, bouncing on the toes of her sling-back pumps.

"Yes," Sydney replied truthfully. He looked like the perfect bookend for Francie. The two of them could get together and make happy, superhero babies—beautiful, bright-eyed tots who could blast through rock with their laser-beam smiles. "You should go talk to him."

"Right. Yeah." Francie nodded, her expression a mixture of giddy anticipation and sheer terror. "I'm going to go to the bathroom."

"Uh . . . that doesn't sound like a logical way to meet Logical Guy," Sydney pointed out.

"I just want to primp a bit." She grabbed Sydney's handbag and opened it. "Can I borrow your brush? I couldn't fit mine in my purse. Oh, and could I use your lipstick? My color got all wiped off when we ate those cheese sticks at the refreshment table. Which reminds me . . . Do you have any breath mints or gum?" Sydney's arm jostled violently as Francie burrowed through the main pouch.

"Here. Just take the whole purse." Sydney slid the strap down her arm and pressed the bag into Francie's hands.

Francie looked appalled. "I can't walk around with two purses. I'd look weird."

"Put yours inside it. That way you'll have whatever you need."

"Hey, yeah." Francie stowed her itty-bitty bag into Sydney's larger one. "Thanks."

Sydney smiled. "No problem. Now go! Go get Logical Guy!"

"Thanks, Syd," Francie gave her a look of sincere gratitude before turning and disappearing into the crowd.

Sydney slunk over to lean against a large oak armoire and yanked her fingers until the knuckles popped. With no one to talk to and no purse to fiddle with, she felt awkward and irrelevant. For the first time, she could understand why people took up smoking.

It occurred to her that she should mingle. But unlike Francie, she'd never been good at approaching strangers. Especially at a party.

It was truly mystifying. For some reason, there seemed to be an inverse correlation between the number of people gathered and the intelligence level of a conversation. Get two people together and they could open up like long-lost soul mates. A handful of people might manage frank, interesting discussions of politics, religion, or the basic state of mankind. But a houseful of college kids seemed capable only of high-fiving each other every two minutes and shouting, *"Dude!"*

From her hunched position next to the cabinet, she had a clear view of the nearby dining room. The bulk of the guests seemed to be congregated there, gathered around something like bees swarming a hive. Looking closer, she realized they were surrounding a large beer keg.

Just then, a guy caught her eye. A tall blond whose jeans looked so crisp and clean, she wondered if he'd ironed them along with his white designer button-down. As she watched, the guy broke from the pack and started walking over to her.

"Hi," he said. His features were drawn together in an almost shy expression, but his body language was bold. He moved right into her personal space and rested his hand on the wall beside her head. "Can I get you a beer?"

"No. I'm just waiting for my friend." She hadn't meant to sound so unfriendly, but her words came out shrill and jumpy, and she instinctively shrank back from his presence.

The guy shrugged and strode away.

Five minutes later another guy approached. "Hey. Wan'a beer?"

She shook her head. "No."

He flashed her a "whatever" look and moved on to another girl.

Barely three minutes after that came bachelor

number three in a makeshift toga: "Hey, you! How about a beer?"

You have got to be kidding me, she thought. Was this the standard pickup line? Or did she just look really thirsty?

She smiled weakly and shook her head. "I'm fine. Thanks anyway."

The guy took a step forward, stumbling on the blue-striped bedsheet he had draped over his T-shirt and jeans. "Aw, come on! What's wrong?" he asked, his Miller High Life breath hitting her full in the face with every word. "You don't like beer?"

She sighed wearily. A mini fantasy of her telling him the whole, unvarnished truth rolled through her mind. *No, I like beer. I prefer fine red wines, but I'll drink an imported lager now and then. Unfortunately I have an important briefing in the morning with top CIA officials concerning a highly classified and extremely dangerous mission, so I really need to keep my wits about me.*

Tempting, but unwise.

She decided to try a new strategy. "Oh, I like beer," she said, blinking innocently. "In fact, my *boyfriend* already went to get me one. You might know him. Vic? He's about your height but bigger on account of all the steroids and bodybuilding. He should be back any second."

Toga guy took a quick step backward, nearly tripping on the gathered corner of the sheet. "Oh. Okay," he said, his wide eyes roving about the room. "I was . . . just checking." Then he turned and stumbled off in the opposite direction.

Sydney sighed and swallowed hard. She really was thirsty.

She squeezed through the packed dining room into the kitchen. Party-goers were in every corner, a few even sitting on the countertops. One guy stood in front of the refrigerator, tossing sandwich fixings over his shoulder to his buddy by the butcher's block. Sydney peered past him, searching the fridge for a soda. The only liquid she could see was a half-empty bottle of Tabasco sauce.

Sydney was just about to fill a glass with tap water when she spotted a large galvanized washtub, an empty can of pineapple-orange juice, and two empty bottles of ginger ale on a nearby counter. A few tiny remnants of ice cubes floated in the tub's frothy yellow contents.

She took a green plastic tumbler out of a cupboard and filled it with the large metal ladle. Then she took a sip. The punch was really good. Sweet and fruity and fizzy. She tipped back the cup and drained it in seconds, then refilled her glass.

"Hi." A guy seemed to materialize next to her. He

was smiling and bobbing his head to the Red Hot Chili Peppers song on the stereo. "Hey, can I get you a—"

"No!" she replied a little more emphatically than she'd planned. "I mean . . . it's okay," she said, holding up her cup, "I've already got some punch."

His mouth stretched into a knowing grin. "I gotcha," he said, nodding even faster. The movement was making her dizzy. "Goin' for the hard stuff tonight, huh?"

"What?" Sydney sniffed her cup suspiciously.

The guy laughed. "No, man. It's tequila. My buddy Greg poured in two bottles. You can't smell it when it's mixed with all that juice and stuff."

Sydney's eyes widened. *Oh, no. Oh, no no no!* Had she actually stayed away from the keg all night just to end up slurping down hard liquor? Suddenly she felt flushed.

Sure enough, the effects were starting to kick in full force. Her body seemed softer, floppier. And every action required a little more effort, as if she were moving underwater. Even her mind had lost its sharp edge. Her brain kept swerving around like a rusty bumper car, letting thoughts randomly ram into her instead of following a distinct path. Stupid, stupid. How could she have let this happen? Didn't she supposedly work in *intelligence?*

Work . . . Oh, god. A new, unsettling realization

blindsided her: She had that critical SD-6 briefing in the morning. She could lose her job because of some guy named Greg!

"So . . ." The guy leaned toward her, placing his hand against the wall. "You want to go for a walk or something?"

Or *something?* Did this doofus really think he was going to get lucky? Sydney pressed her fingers to her temples and closed her eyes. This was a new low. She was drunk, miserable, surrounded by annoying people, and risking life and career by blowing off her studies. Why did she ever agree to come to this awful party?

"I think I'm going to be sick," she muttered.

In one quick, jerky movement the guy pulled his arm away and stepped back, a wary look creasing his features. Sydney tried hard not to laugh. She hadn't meant the statement literally. But as long as it was working . . .

She let her face go completely slack and pressed her hand over her mouth. "Will you excuse me?" she mumbled through her fingers.

"Uh . . . yeah. Yeah, sure," the guy replied, flattening himself against the paneling to allow maximum space for her escape route.

Sydney stumbled past him and tossed her nearly empty tumbler of punch into the sink. Then she fumbled with the brass handle of the patio door until it finally opened, pulling her through to the tiled terrace beyond.

She leaned against the stucco exterior wall and inhaled the crisp night air. At last she was outside. Outside the house and outside the scene.

It was where she belonged.

* * *

Breathe in. . . . Breathe out. . . . Breathe in. . . . Breathe . . . out? Or was she at the in part again?

Forget it, Sydney thought, slouching against a cast-iron bench. Breathing was just too hard. Luckily a nippy ocean wind was keeping people indoors, and she had the entire patio to herself. No one around to see her gasping like a beached guppy.

She still had to find a way to sober up, though. Maybe she could somehow work the alcohol out of her system. Of course, she couldn't exactly do a few laps around the block in her high heels. But maybe Lover Boy was right about her needing a walk.

She stood a little too quickly, causing her vision to tilt and swirl. Reaching back, she grasped hold of the bench and steadied herself.

God, she hated this. She'd only been drunk twice before. Once, a few months earlier when she hadn't known her margarita limit and got sick. And the other, the very first time, when she was fifteen. She'd invited a friend to sleep over and the girl had talked Sydney into breaking into her dad's liquor cabinet. They'd tried a lot of stuff they didn't like and then ended up chugging a bottle of warm chardonnay. They'd giggled for about half an hour and then passed out into their pillows. She'd caught hell from her nanny the next day, and she'd never hung out much with the school pal after that. Amazingly enough, she'd kept her fondness for fine wines, only now she tried to restrict herself to two glasses.

Gradually, Sydney's sight realigned itself and she was able to gaze around the lush backyard. These Sigma Freud guys had quite a spread. She'd seen city parks smaller than this. They had a swimming pool, blacktop, volleyball pit, tetherball pole, and a long grassy stretch that extended to the next block. She could barely make out a small grove of oak trees and an aluminum garden shed in the distance.

Maybe she could stroll inside the fence line a couple of times until her head cleared. That way she wouldn't have to leave Francie or beg her to go home in the middle of her fun.

She started walking, tracing the circumference of the yard. The downward slope of the grounds quickened her step and made her lean forward slightly onto her toes. After a while, the earth beneath the grass became moist and sticky, as if it had been recently watered, and she had to yank upward at the knee in order to dislodge the heels of her shoes. Anyone watching from a distance would have thought she'd broken into a clumsy military march.

The noises of the party had almost completely dwindled. There was only the throbbing bass beat of the stereo and an occasional high-pitched shriek of laughter. The rest had died down to a distant hum that blended into the sighs of the wind and the swishing sounds of nearby highway traffic.

Sydney focused on the sluggish rhythm of her heartbeat echoing in her ears. Already her head felt a little clearer, and she hadn't even completed one lap yet. She made a deal with herself. She would finish this go-round, do one more, and then go into the house and tell Francie she had to leave. After that, she would return to her egghead existence and put her partying days behind her.

She made her way past the cluster of oak trees in the northeast corner of the yard. The barks were covered with different-colored splatters of Day-Glo paint, probably from past paintball battles, and someone's blue boxer shorts were hanging from a low branch.

"If these trees could talk," she murmured, shaking her head.

A new noise suddenly cut through the air. Sydney stopped. A faint moan was coming through the trees.

"I was just kidding," she said to the nearest trunk.

It sounded again. Sydney cocked her head and listened. It wasn't the trees at all. A high-pitched yelping noise, like a hurt puppy, was coming from behind the garden shed in the opposite back corner of the yard. She stalked forward to investigate, still wobbling slightly on the damp grass.

After a few feet she stumbled upon a brick walkway leading directly to the shed. Sydney followed it around to the side of the structure. The noise was louder now, and she recognized it as a female voice—a *sobbing* female voice.

"No! No!" the girl whimpered.

Her sobs were joined by a second voice. This one low and raspy. "Come on," it said, followed by an incomprehensible mumble.

Sydney was too tipsy and too focused on the sounds to notice that her feet were continuing to propel her forward. Before she realized it, she was rounding the back corner of the shed.

Two shapes loomed in front of her in the dim light. A flaxen-haired girl was crouched in a half-sitting position against the rear wall. Sydney could tell she was drunk—much drunker than she herself was. Her clothes were rumpled, makeup was smudged across her face, and it looked as if she could barely hold herself upright. A lineman-sized guy loomed over her. As Sydney watched, he muttered something to the girl and tried to cup her face in one of his hands, but she kept moaning and shaking her head back and forth. The movement caused her to slide downward almost to the ground. The guy seized her roughly and slammed her back against the wall, pressing himself against her to keep her from falling.

The girl cried out and began sobbing louder.

"Shut up," the guy growled.

"Leave her alone!" Sydney shouted, stepping forward unsteadily.

The guy let go of the girl and whirled around. Sydney felt as surprised as he looked. Okay, so now they knew she was there. What exactly was she going to do?

He straightened up to full height and looked Sydney up and down. A ragged smirk stole across his face. The girl crumpled onto her knees, hugging herself and sobbing.

"What did you say?" he asked, moving toward Sydney, his hulking form shielding what little light she had to go by.

"I said leave her alone," Sydney repeated.

The guy started laughing hoarsely. "Or you'll what?"

Sydney paused. She hadn't really figured that out yet. She'd been sort of playing it by ear with that bumper-car brain of hers. Actually, she could do a lot of things. A hard elbow to his sternum came to mind. But then she'd never really tried her street-fighting skills while drunk. She might not actually have the upper hand on him.

No, it would be better to try a different tack altogether.

"Or I'll go call the cops," she answered, raising her chin defiantly.

The guy's wheezy chuckles ceased abruptly. Staggering forward, he grabbed Sydney's wrist and yanked her toward him. "You are in way over your head," he growled.

Something snapped in Sydney's mind, like a harness breaking. Before she realized it, she'd wrenched herself out of his grasp and whirled her leg around as hard as she could. She felt her shinbone collide with something, but the movement sent her spinning around wildly.

Eventually she stopped turning. She fixed her gaze forward and blinked a few times, as if hitting a mental tracking button. Her surroundings zoomed back into focus, but there was no sign of the big guy. She stepped forward to investigate and promptly stumbled on something. Looking down, she saw that it was him. The jerk had apparently fallen flat against the brick pavers and was knocked out cold.

All of a sudden, a piercing scream sounded next to her, searing her nerves like a heavy dose of electricity. The girl sat rocking back and forth, hugging her knees to her chest. Her eyes were glued to the guy's unconscious form and her mouth was wide open, letting forth a series of high-decibel shrieks.

Sydney glanced around wildly. The porch lights had been switched on, and already a few confused-looking party-goers were stepping onto the terrace and squinting into the darkness.

Now what? How would she explain? She glanced about her, hoping a brilliant idea would hit her head-on.

Her eyes locked onto the ivy-covered chain-link fence. She charged forward and leaped onto it, pulling herself up and over. The sharp tines of the top knots pinched her palms and she could hear the lining of her dress rip, but she forced herself to keep on.

A second later, she plummeted to the sidewalk below. Sydney looked around her, grabbed a shoe in each hand, and took off running.

4

SYDNEY GLANCED DOWN AT her silver-tone Bugs Bunny watch. According to Bugs's gloved hands, it was almost midnight.

She should be home in bed dreaming in Romanian after having spent hours studying vocabulary like a dutiful secret agent. But she hadn't done that. And she wasn't dutiful. She was a sorry, drunken excuse for an operative.

She couldn't believe she'd actually done Krav Maga on the jerk at the party. Not that he didn't deserve it, but *still*. There must have been a better way of handling it. Maybe Noah was right about her reacting without thinking.

She wondered what had happened after she left. Maybe the hysterical girl gave a detailed account of the entire episode. Maybe the cops were after her. She hoped they'd be more interested in locking up the sleazeball guy. Or maybe they'd want to track her down to give her a medal? Either way, it could end up being a gigantic breach of SD-6 security. And from what she understood, breaches were dealt with severely. In other words, permanently.

And what about Francie? Did she know what had happened? If so, how would Sydney explain it? If not, what reason could she give for having deserted her at the party? She could only hope Francie was okay and not too mad at her.

Unnh. Sydney massaged her temples. Her brain hurt from thinking, and her mouth was completely dry. All she wanted was to feel normal again. What she really needed, what she'd give just about anything for at that moment, was a hot, steaming cup of coffee.

She rounded the corner and came to a complete halt. There, fifteen yards in front of her, stood a small, brightly lit convenience store. She squinted at the glowing, molded red plastic lettering over the entrance. THE STOP-BUY, it read. Venturing closer, she could see the hours of operation sign next to the door. Closing time was midnight, and according to Bugs, it was five minutes till.

Sydney dashed inside. "Excuse me," she said to the person behind the counter. "Do you have—?"

The cashier rose to face her and she stopped short, the words dissolving in her throat. Burke Wells was smiling at her from the other side of the laminate countertop.

"Hey," he said. "Sydney, isn't it?"

She closed her eyes for a split second and then re-opened them, as if the picture might change if she just blinked hard enough. But he was still there. Still grinning. Deep dimples appeared just below his side-burns.

"Um . . . I was just . . ." She swallowed hard. How to begin? "I was wondering if you had some coffee," she finished finally.

His blue-green eyes sagged apologetically. "Sorry. We're about to close and I just finished cleaning the machine."

"Oh." A feeling of disappointment so intense spilled through her, she actually felt like crying. She had so wanted that coffee. But it wasn't just the coffee. It was the running and the tequila and Noah's harsh words and her quite possible looming execution. It was so unfair. After all, if she was going to be put to death soon, didn't she at least deserve coffee?

"Are you okay?" Burke asked, his red-blond eyebrows bunching together.

Sydney glanced down at herself. She was pretty pitiful. Muddy high heels, bedraggled hair, and a jagged piece of lining poking out from under the hem of her dress. She looked like a transient parade queen.

"What happened?" he asked. "Hot date gone bad?"

Sydney gave a quick shrug. She couldn't talk. She was afraid if she tried to utter a word, she might end up blubbering right there in front of him.

"You sure you're going to be all right?" Burke asked softly.

His concern disarmed her. Hot tears swam in front of her eyes and her lips began an involuntary quiver. Sydney quickly clapped her hands over her face and pretended to yawn. "I'm okay," she mumbled into her palms. She rubbed her eyes with the tips of her fingers. "I just need something to . . . clear my head," she added.

Burke regarded her for a moment. "You know," he said, "I've got just the thing." He nimbly leaped over the counter, keys and loose change jingling in the pockets of his faded utility pants, and walked to the front of the store. There he locked the door, partially lowered the outer steel gate, and pulled the short chain of the neon Open sign, switching it off.

Sydney leaned against the checkout counter,

watching Burke head down the center aisle toward the back of the store. *Whatever magical cure Burke has in store for me, I sure hope it's strong,* she prayed silently. Images of some green, herbal sludge popped up in her head, causing her to scrunch her nose instinctively. Still, she'd try anything at this point.

"You're in luck," he called out from behind a tall, pyramid-shaped stack of soft drink cases. "We got a fresh shipment in today." A second later he rounded the corner.

He held up his hand and Sydney was relieved to see that it wasn't some holistic, vegetable-based elixir at all, but a round, pint-sized container of . . .

"Ice cream?" she exclaimed as he set the frost-covered carton on the counter beside her.

"The perfect remedy for a night of overindulgence," he said, patting the lid. "Am I right in guessing you've let yourself . . . get a little carried away with stuff?"

You have no idea, she thought. "Maybe," she conceded aloud. "But ice cream won't work. It'll melt before I get home."

"Then eat it now."

"Here?"

"Why not?" His shoulders lifted, grazing the bottom of his hair.

"But . . . but . . ." She took a breath and waited

for some obvious, primary-level logic to smack her upside the head. "But I have nothing to eat it with," she finished lamely.

"I can fix that." He walked past her toward the fountain drink and condiment area and grabbed a thick plastic spoon. "Problem solved," he said, holding it up.

Sydney could feel her defenses caving, withering from the lack of electrolytes in her blood. Besides, she had to admit, chocolate ice cream did sound really, really good.

"Okay," she said, sounding like a six-year-old agreeing to eat her lima beans. "How much is it?" She absently reached for her purse and realized, in horror, that Francie still had it.

Burke waved a hand. "Don't worry about it. It's on me. In fact," he added, pulling out another spoon. "How about I join you?"

* * *

"It's '62."

"No, it's '60."

"I'm telling you, I've seen *Lawrence of Arabia* twelve times and it came out in '62."

They sat on the floor with their backs against the front counter. Sydney's legs were curled underneath her, her shoes in a heap by the candy display. Burke's frayed sneaker bounced on his raised left knee as he cupped the ice cream carton in one hand while scooping out a large spoonful with the other.

He deposited it in his mouth and pointed the empty spoon at her. "Are you sure?" he asked between chews. "I always thought it was 1960."

Sydney smiled. After scarfing down over two and a half pints of chocolate chocolate-chip with Burke, the storm clouds in her head had finally dispersed—along with the nagging pounding. It felt good being able to access her intelligence again. "I'm positive. It premiered in the U.S. and Great Britain in December 1962. Although David Lean was probably doing pre-production work in '60," she added generously.

She wasn't sure how they'd gotten on this topic. She'd made some hyperbolic statement about her throat being as dry as the desert, which led to him making some vague reference to the movie, at which she disclosed that it was her favorite film of all time, which began a whole spate of reenactments of scenes and dialogue, and then eventually his argument about the release date.

He passed her the carton and licked a stray drop from his finger. "That's cool that you know so much about movies."

"Well . . ." She cocked a shoulder and grinned in spite of herself. "I'm not exactly an expert."

"I once mentioned David Lean to this friend of mine, and he thought I was talking about the guy who made *Blue Velvet.* Then, when I pointed out that was actually David Lynch, he just looked at me and said, 'Whatever.' Like they were interchangeable or something. As if a first name is close enough. Michael Jordan or Michael Jackson? Whatever. George Bush or George Burns? Whatever."

Sydney leaned her head against the counter wall and laughed.

"I mean, I don't mean to sound like a snob, but I do believe in accuracy."

"Yeah. Me too."

They lapsed into an easy silence. She continued to scrape the ice cream with the tip of her spoon, trying to uncover hidden chocolate chunks, while he checked his fingers for more drips.

It was as if she were with Francie, only different. Maybe it was the traces of liquor in her system. Or maybe it was the way Burke reminded her of Robert Redford in *Butch Cassidy and the Sundance Kid.* Whatever it was, she felt an undeniable snugness that allowed her to be more open than usual. There was even a moment, while giggling at one of his stories, when she'd had the urge to lay her head against his shoulder. Nothing brazen or flirtatious, just a need to make the connection she was feeling physical in some way. She'd probably have wanted to grab his hand if hers wasn't so sticky.

What exactly was happening? What was behind all this? Did she like him? Well, of course she liked him. But did she *like* him?

She discreetly studied his profile as she scraped the side of the container. Burke was definitely gorgeous. Smart, too. Not to mention fun, in a goofy sort of way. And yet her heart didn't exactly do calisthenics around him. She did feel something, though. Something she couldn't quite identify.

Maybe she should just investigate further, use some of her hard-earned covert-ops training.

"So . . . why do you like *Lawrence of Arabia* so much?" she asked, handing back the ice cream.

Burke frowned slightly as he considered. "I don't know. I guess I always liked how T. E. Lawrence did things on his own terms."

"Yeah, I know. That's exactly why I like it," she said, nodding. "Well, that and seeing young Peter O'Toole with a desert tan."

He burst out laughing. "Aha! The truth comes out!"

Sydney watched him, smiling. Every time Burke laughed it surprised her. Not because he found her funny—which was surprising in itself—but because it made him seem so . . . normal. She'd always thought of Burke as a figurehead, the radical campus archetype. But his laugh exposed him as being completely, adorably human.

Burke's laugh was more guttural than vocal. His chin lifted, his shoulders jiggled, and seal-like sounds rose from his throat. It was a naked sort of laugh; the type of laugh a person only used with lifelong best friends. Sydney could feel herself melting along with the chocolate chocolate-chip.

She opened her mouth to say something, then shut it and shook her head.

"What?" he asked, noticing.

"Nothing." She glanced down at the gold-flecked floor tiles.

"No, really," he added, scooting around to face her. "Say anything. I believe in total honesty. It's why I'm so down on governments and corporations all the time. They're always lying to people." He opened his arms as if presenting himself. "Go ahead. I've got nothing to hide. Tell me whatever it was you were thinking."

"When do you have time to do something as frivolous as see a movie? I assumed you'd be too busy staging sit-ins and circulating petitions."

He laughed again. "No, I do have a sliver of a social life," he said. "I mean, no one can be all about work or school or fighting for good causes, right?"

Sydney's grin faltered slightly. "Right," she said, as if it were the most obvious thing in the world. Inwardly, though, she couldn't help wondering: What else did *she* have? Other than her best friendship with Francie, her life was pretty much defined by events at work and school.

She'd assumed Burke was just like her—perpetually on a mission. But even he managed to fit into social scenes. He probably never ran away terrified from a party, either. Burke was, in fact, nothing like she had thought. She got the feeling that he was actually revealing his true self, that he truly did believe in complete honesty. People like him were rare.

"So . . . what happened?" he asked, tilting his head toward her.

"What?"

"Why'd you abandon your date tonight?"

"Oh." Sydney's cheeks suddenly felt sunburned. "Things didn't turn out the way I hoped." She grasped the torn piece of lining sticking out from her skirt and slowly twisted it.

"Hmm." Burke nodded solemnly. He set the ice cream down on the floor and tilted his head close to hers. "Are you going to be okay?"

A crop of tiny goose bumps sprouted along her arm. "Yeah," she said, looking over at him. "I will."

"If there's anything I can do, just say it. I don't

believe in violence, but I *do* believe in justice. With one phone call I can have twelve guys camped out on his front lawn with picket signs."

Sydney chuckled. "No. That won't be necessary. But thanks anyway."

She glanced down at her torn lining and began winding it up in the other direction. It was funny how Burke assumed she'd been having boyfriend trouble. After all, to have boyfriend trouble, one needed a boyfriend. Which she didn't have. Which she never did. She was, however, in lots of trouble. The type of trouble that couldn't be solved by protesters with signs.

"Well, one thing's for sure," Burke said, tossing the empty ice cream container into the nearby trash can.

"What's that?" she asked, accepting his hand and letting him pull her to a standing position.

"You need a ride home."

"No, that's all right. I can walk." She grabbed hold of the counter while slipping her feet into her shoes.

Burke shook his head. "I don't think so. It's late and dark. Besides, there's lots of frat houses in this area and their parties can get kind of out of hand."

Sydney opened her mouth to protest and then quickly shut it. What could she say? *Don't worry. I know how to handle those guys. I just clip them so hard they end up drooling on the pavement.*

"Come on," Burke insisted. "Let me give you a ride."

She paused, pretending to adjust her outfit as she considered. Why exactly was she hesitating? It wasn't as if she *wanted* to walk twelve blocks in her two-inch heels. And it wasn't that she didn't trust Burke. She somehow did—completely. So was it because letting a guy take you home usually stood for something? Would it mean something to Burke? To her?

She reached up and rubbed the skin between her brows. What exactly was she doing? Was she thinking about her feelings or deciding how she felt about her thoughts? She didn't know anymore. She was just very, very tired.

All the more reason to get home as soon as possible.

"Sure. I'll take a ride," she replied, smiling. "Thanks."

She rubbed her upper arms as she stood on the sidewalk waiting for him to lock the doors. The wind had picked up speed and was now the same temperature as the ice cream in the pit of her stomach. As they walked down the sidewalk, Burke gave her his battered army-green windbreaker. He didn't turn it into a grand gesture of chivalry—simply dropped it on her shoulders and draped it over her arms. She accepted it without argument. Wondering if it was a big deal might make it a big deal, and she really didn't want to over-analyze anything. Besides, she was cold.

They veered around the corner of the store. "My chariot awaits," Burke said, making a sweeping gesture with his arm. Under the glow of a bug-swarmed streetlamp stood a dark blue bike.

"You're giving me a ride on a bicycle?" she asked incredulously.

"Sure. Why not?" He loped over to the bike and unlocked the chain holding it to the light pole. He slipped the chain into his backpack; then he shouldered the pack and kicked off. After a slow circle around the empty parking lot, he coasted toward Sydney and stopped inches from her feet. "Hop on," he said, patting the crossbar.

He's got to be kidding, she thought, eyeing the hard metal pole.

Burke let out one of his deep, throaty laughs. "Come on. I promise I won't go too fast. Here, look." He reached into his pack and pulled out a yellow T-shirt that read *Corporate Subsidies—the Real Welfare* and wrapped it around the bar. "There. Now you'll have some extra padding."

"Ohh-kay," she said with a shrug.

She slid her arms into Burke's jacket, stepped up to the bike, and sat down on the makeshift cushion, figuring that riding sidesaddle would be the most comfortable—and modest—position to be in. Burke placed his hands on the handlebars, trapping her with his lean, muscular arms.

"Are you ready?" he asked.

"I guess," she said resignedly. "But remember this: If you try any wheelies, I'll break your ribs." She was only half joking.

Burke laughed again. This time she could feel the tremors behind his breastbone. "I promise I won't. So where to?"

"Up this street to Sunset. Then four blocks down."

They took off. Burke eased the turn onto the street in order to keep the bike as upright as possible. Once they were on the open road, they gained momentum until they reached an easy glide. The cool night wind rushed past her, whipping her skirt about her legs and causing locks of hair to rise in a jerky sort of dance.

It was exhilarating. At first Sydney tried to hold herself as rigid as possible. Eventually she found it easier to balance by leaning back against Burke, nestling herself in the crook of his left shoulder. This allowed her to hold her legs out away from the front wheel.

She could feel his breath near her ear where it mingled with the night air, and smell his spicy scent of sweat and exotic incense. Was it her imagination or was he leaning forward, curving his shoulders around her? For once, she didn't care. She didn't tense up, and her mind didn't fly into hyperanalysis. She simply relaxed against him.

She still had to deal with Francie, SD-6, and the ramifications of her actions. But at least for now, she was okay. For now, she could just close her eyes and enjoy the ride.

To: bossman@creditdauphine.com
From: reginald.wilson@creditdauphine.com
Subject: Sydney

This could be a mistake. We could lose
her.

To: reginald.wilson@creditdauphine.com
From: bossman@creditdauphine.com
Subject: Re: Sydney

She won't fail. We need her. She needs
this.
Mission to move forward as scheduled.

5

BE-BEEP! BE-BEEP! BE-BEEP! BE-BEEP!

Sydney gasped and sat upright. Peach-colored light flooded in through her dorm window, spearing her pupils. A thousand-decibel alarm was blaring.

"Francie, get up. I think there's a fire," she tried to say, only her voice came out croaky, unintelligible. Francie continued to sleep soundly—not even the slightest flutter in her thick, dark lashes.

BE-BEEP! BE-BEEP! BE-BEEP!

The noise was coming from her nightstand. Sydney shielded her eyes against the blinding morning light with one hand and groped along the tabletop with the other. Her fingers eventually closed on a small, vibrating rectangle. Her pager.

Stupid thing must be malfunctioning, she thought. *It's never been this loud before.*

She grasped the box and fumbled with the row of tiny buttons until it finally stopped wailing. Then she turned it over and squinted down at the alphanumeric display screen. WILSON—9:00 it read.

"The briefing," she mumbled as she slipped out from under the covers and stood up straight, her temples throbbing from the change in altitude.

Oh well, she thought. *At least I don't have to worry about SD-6 executing me.*

After Burke had seen her into the lobby the night before, she'd come upstairs to find Francie pacing the room. The minute she saw Sydney she began apologizing profusely. "I'm so sorry I didn't wait for you when I was running from the cops!" Gradually, Sydney was able to cobble together a version of what had happened after she left: A neighbor called the police when the girl screamed; the jerk came to and told everyone he'd been beaten up by a guy—or maybe two; the girl had been too drunk to remember anything; and as soon as everyone heard sirens, all the underage drinkers took off running.

Francie assumed Sydney had done the same thing and realized halfway home that she had Sydney's wallet. "I'm just so glad the cops didn't stop you," she'd said to Sydney.

That makes two of us, she had thought before collapsing into bed.

Of course, she wasn't completely out of hot water. Wilson could have heard about everything that happened. Since she still wasn't a fully trained agent, it was possible SD-6 had someone tailing her.

She could only imagine the report Wilson might get. *Subject seen doing clumsy roundhouse kick on 285-pound party-goer. Subject then seen jumping chain-link fence like frightened squirrel. Soon after, subject observed eating and talking with known antigovernment radical.*

Not exactly a page lifted from a career improvement book. And it would be especially upsetting considering the confidence they were placing in her with this upcoming mission.

And what if Noah found out? came a voice inside her pounding head. *What would he say?*

"Shut up," she said to the voice. She couldn't even think about that now.

What she needed to think about was a long, hot shower and gallons of coffee. Maybe she should even shower in the coffee.

As she headed for the bathroom, her gaze passed over the bedside clock. Almost immediately her head snapped back for a second look—a move that seemed to dislodge her frontal lobes. It was already 8:37.

"No!" she moaned. She had no time for a shower *or* coffee. She barely had time to change.

If she wasn't careful, this could end up being a very, very bad day.

* * *

"Balfour Isle is three miles long and one mile wide."

Sydney focused on the grainy satellite image on the screen.

"It's twenty miles off the west coast of Scotland and approximately thirty miles from international waters," Wilson went on.

Sydney tried to look alert. She'd been so relieved when she arrived at work and realized no one knew about her lapses in judgment. But relief had been replaced by guilt. Here they were, handing her a crucial life-and-death mission, and she had to force herself not to fall face forward. Maybe she didn't deserve their trust after all.

"If you turn to page four in your assignment notebook, you'll see that your entry plans are standard procedure." Wilson pressed the control panel and all the video screens in the conference room went blank.

As her computer faded, Sydney caught sight of

her reflection on the monitor. Her hair was sticking out at strange angles, and a thin layer of grease shone on her unwashed face. She'd told Wilson when she arrived that she'd gone for a long jog that morning, to help explain why she looked like an electroshock therapy patient. He'd bought it without question—which made her feel even more lame. She'd never lied to him before.

Sydney leaned forward and flipped to the page in her notebook, glad for a reason to move. As she scanned the date and time of her flight and connecting train and the address of her contacts in Edinburgh, she couldn't help thinking that this time there would be no Noah to guide her or chastise her. She'd be alone, completely cut off from her fellow agents, her reliable technology, her country, and her old life. It would be as if she had disappeared.

Which might not be *too* bad . . .

It could be kind of refreshing to go solo. Relying only on herself. No distractions, going on instinct and training alone.

In which case I should probably stop daydreaming and read, she scolded herself, staring back down at the timetable.

"According to intelligence sources," Wilson said, "the list of people who have RSVP'd to von Muller's summit meeting are you and four others: Carmina

Polito, a representative of Mercado de Sangre; Konstantin Baranov of K-Directorate; Nigel Hubbard, whose UK-based outfit runs arms and drugs throughout Europe and parts of Asia; and Asam Rifat, a Turk whose Red Star ring openly competes with Hubbard's business. Nichita would not have ever dealt with these individuals in person. But you should still study some of their past records as detailed in your notobook."

Sydney nodded along obediently. "Okay."

"Now then," Wilson glanced up from the mosaic of charts and reports scattered in front of him and met her gaze. "I know you told me at our last briefing that you were up for this mission. But even though we've already used some manpower in setting up this assignment, it isn't too late if you've changed your mind."

He paused for a few beats, studying her. "I have to repeat that this is going to be highly dangerous for you, Sydney," he went on. "You will basically be flying solo, without a net. Are you sure . . . are you *absolutely positive* that you want to do this?"

Sydney rummaged through her emotions. Was she sure? He made it sound so dire. Impossible even. Could she really handle this?

"Yes." The minute she said it, she knew she believed it. She could definitely do this. If there was anything she was good at, it was relying only on herself. In fact, it might be easier than having another agent around looking out for you, criticizing your every move—and possibly even turning on you.

Wilson remained silent for a moment. "All right then," he said. He leaned over and pressed a button on his phone. "Graham? Could you come in here now, please?"

Sydney sat forward expectantly. She'd heard all about Graham, their op-tech specialist. Apparently he was a whiz at inventing and modifying all sorts of gadgets and weapons. Now she would finally get to meet him.

The door opened and a tall, gangly guy walked in, carrying a shiny steel attaché.

Sydney had expected a man, but she'd envisioned someone older. Graham looked like a college student—then Sydney noticed his Scooby Doo T-shirt and *Star Trek* belt buckle—or younger.

He stood at the front of the table and cleared his throat. Wispy black hair framed his pale face, and his brown eyes were magnified by heavy-framed glasses.

"Because of the mandates of this mission I wasn't able to create tools to the best of my abilities," he said quietly. "In fact, I had to resort to almost caveman-like devices.

"However, I did manage to construct two useful

and, dare I say, ingenious devices that should remain undetected during the search and sensor sweep." He paused for effect.

"We do appreciate the effort you've put in on this case," Wilson remarked, sounding a little impatient. "Please show us what you've brought."

Graham set his briefcase on the table and opened it. "This first apparatus resembles a pair of ordinary sunglasses," he said, handing the device to Sydney. "But the lenses are made out of special diachronic glass. After dark, you should stare at the sweeps from the nearby lighthouse. The lenses will filter out all light except for the part of the spectrum your team will bury in the beam as a Morse code message. This way, we can get information to you. You won't be able to contact us."

Sydney looked them over, hoping the hasty Morse code lessons she'd undergone were good enough.

Graham reached back inside the case and held up a black satin and lace bustier. "This looks like ordinary lingerie," he went on, his cheeks turning the color of cocktail shrimp, "but hidden inside the boning is actually a steel-and-wire harness. If your contacts on the mainland detect a problem and want you to abort the mission, they will signal an emergency pickup. You should then remove the harness, put it on, and get to the roof parapet. A helicopter will then fly over, lower a hook to attach to the harness, and lift you off to safety. Got it?" he asked, his cheeks fading back to white.

"Got it." Sydney tried not to smile as she thought of Graham fashioning a black lace corset.

"Any other weapons or tools that you need will have to be fashioned out of your surroundings," Wilson said as Graham left the room. "You depart in two days. We have arranged for your aunt Lila to become extremely ill, requiring you to miss classes to be by her side."

"But . . . I don't have an Aunt Lila."

"You do now, along with all the necessary physicians' notes to show to your professors."

"Right," Sydney said slowly, still amazed at how quickly SD-6 could get things done. She'd legitimately tried to get a doctor's note once for strep throat, and it had taken weeks.

Wilson rose from his seat and Sydney followed suit. "In the meantime, step up your hand-to-hand training and keep studying your Romanian."

"Okay."

"And Sydney?"

She paused in front of the door. "Yes?"

Wilson walked over and placed his large, weighty hand on her shoulder. "Don't worry.

Everything's going to be fine," he said. "I know we can count on you."

* * *

She made it ten feet down the corridor before running into Noah.

"I need to talk to you," he said, falling into step beside her.

"Save it." She kept her gaze focused forward, allowing her sudden burst of anger to quicken her pace.

"Come on, Sydney."

Oh, so *now* he wanted to be on a first-name basis. After making her feel like a pesky four-year-old and then slamming her in front of her boss. She stopped abruptly and narrowed her eyes at him. "I don't have anything to say."

To her ever-mounting frustration, he smiled. "Then just hear me out."

Sydney squeezed her eyes shut and exhaled loudly.

"Come on, Syd. It'll just take a moment." His voice was soft.

She opened her eyes and faced him again. "Fine," she said, holding on to her irritation like a lifeline. "You have one minute."

Noah licked his lips and took a breath. "Listen, I really don't think you should go on this mission."

"I know. You made that clear already. You don't think I'm good enough for—"

"No." He shook his head. "That's not it."

"Then why? I don't understand. In Paris we—"

"Shhh!" He held up a hand and glanced up and down the corridor. Then he edged in closer, his face only inches away from hers. "I just don't think it's a good idea," he whispered.

Why was she even listening to him? Why was she still standing there? And why, why, *why* could she not stop staring at that little crevice above his mouth? That smooth channel that sloped from the bottom of his nose to the dip in his upper lip, like a perfectly molded fingerhold?

Because she was pathetic. Whacked. Possibly masochistic. She should go five doors down and sign up for another psych evaluation.

"Why?" she managed to croak, still in the grip of his stare. "You still haven't told me why."

Noah broke off his gaze, turning his head toward the end of the hallway. "I just don't want anything to happen to . . . jeopardize the mission."

Oh. So that was it. He was afraid she'd botch everything up.

"It's too late," she said with all the confidence she

could muster. "It's my op, Agent Hicks. And there's nothing you can say that will change my mind.".

He looked as if he was going to say something. But before he could utter a word, the door across the corridor flew open and a tall, handsome black man walked out holding a bouquet of flowers. Sydney recognized him as the agent she'd smacked into during her very first tour of headquarters last fall.

The agent looked just as surprised as she felt. "Oh. Hi," he said awkwardly. He turned and noticed Noah. "Hey, Hicks."

"Hey, Dixon." Noah ran a hand through his unruly brown hair. The intense earnestness was gone from his face. "Hey, have you met Sydney Bristow? She's one of our latest recruits."

"I'm Marcus Dixon. Nice to meet you." Dixon smiled warmly and extended his empty palm.

"Likewise." As they shook hands, Sydney couldn't help matching his wide, warm smile, in spite of all the excruciating confusion with Noah. His was a genuine, all-out grin—an expression rarely seen in the stuffy corridors of SD-6.

"So what's with the flowers?" Noah nodded toward the bouquet of mixed spring buds. "You trying to butter up Sloane?"

Dixon chuckled. "Not a bad idea, but no. These are for my wife. Our anniversary is today and I'm supposed to meet her for lunch. Which reminds me." His forehead wrinkled sheepishly. "Would you mind seeing if there's any lint on the back of my jacket?" He turned sideways.

Noah picked off a crumb-sized piece of paper and Sydney smoothed a slight pucker in the left shoulder.

"There," she said, with an approving nod. "You're good to go."

"Thanks." He straightened his tie and ran a hand over his closely cropped hair.. "Guess I better be off. Nice to meet you."

Sydney smiled after him as he charged down the hallway. "Wow," she said, shaking her head. "I never thought of these guys as having wives."

"Bad idea."

"What?" She hadn't actually been talking to Noah, but his comment made her spin around and frown at him. "What do you mean?"

Noah shrugged. "Sloane is married, and Dixon is a family guy. But it's a mistake for the rest of us."

"How?"

"This life . . . Agents are too busy to deal with such distractions. And besides," he added, raising an eyebrow, "you never know how long it can go on. Your next mission can always be your last."

He walked backward a few steps, fixing Sydney

with a calculating expression. Then he turned and walked away.

Sydney sighed and hugged her operations note-book to her chest. She wanted to read something into Noah's words, some hidden message he was trying to convey to her. Was it really that he thought she'd screw things up? Or was it remotely possible that he cared what happened to her?

Yeah, right. That's why he insisted she call him Agent Hicks, told Wilson she wasn't prepared, and said marriage was a waste. Because he was so caring.

That's why I've got to stop thinking about Noah, she told herself firmly, trying to focus on Wilson's in-structions. It didn't matter what Noah thought.

It was her mission.

She didn't want it to be her last.

I'm not what you'd call an existentialist. And I'm not exactly a hermit, either. But I have figured out some advantages to going solo. At the top of the list? There's no one there to **rip out your heart** and wring it out like a soggy dishrag.

It's just better to be alone. Because when you let people in, you give them power over you. And in my line of work, you need all the **power** you can get.

6

"**WOULD YOU LIKE SOME** tea or coffee, mum?"

Sydney stared bleary-eyed at the woman standing in the center aisle of the train. Her gaze traveled from the woman's trim, charcoal-colored suit to the gleaming stainless steel decanters on her pushcart. A whiff of French roast spiked the air.

"Coffee would be fantastic." She pushed herself upright and lowered the built-in tray on the back of the seat in front of her.

"Thanks," she said as the woman handed her a steaming cup. She cradled it between her hands, closed her eyes, and took a long, invigorating sip.

After taking an evening flight from LAX to JFK in New York, she'd immediately boarded a flight to London. When she'd left L.A., it had been Thursday. Now it was Friday afternoon and she was on the last leg of the journey—the four-hour express train from London to Edinburgh.

When she first started at SD-6, Sydney had assumed that the element of mortal peril would be the worst part about being an agent. Maybe it was. But all the hours spent sitting in a plane or train were a close second. And then there were the lies. . . . Sydney had given Francie the story about her aunt Lila's double-bypass surgery. In her friend's eyes, she was a saint. *Nah, the lies are definitely the worst part.*

She leaned her head against the plush first-class upholstery and stared out the window, watching as the scenery whizzed past. Ever since the train passed the low stone border of Scotland's Hadrian's Wall, the people and terrain had slowly become more rugged and robust. The colors seemed to have gone through a black dye rinse. The rolling kelly green of the English countryside had gradually been replaced by deeper teals and forest green hues. Sapphire blue waters had turned an inky indigo. And the exposed earth had gone from reddish, velvety chocolate to the color of dark fudge.

She thought briefly of Noah, and then Burke. Burke had called before she left. She'd been careful and guarded, and they'd left off with Burke giving her his phone number. *Not that I'll use it,* she thought. *Or maybe I will?* She shook her head as they sped past an industrial-looking complex. If Noah were a building, he would have a high-tech, barbed-wire security gate, guard dogs foaming at the mouth, and a giant No Soliciting sign. Burke, on the other hand, would be one of those warm, cozy inns you find off the interstate. The old-fashioned kind that smelled of pine needles and baking bread. He'd also have a welcome mat out front and the door would be open wide.

The thing was, she knew more about Burke after an hour or so of conversation than she knew about Noah—even after intensely working alongside him during the Paris mission. But with Noah it had always been something understated. She might not know his favorite movie or political party, but she had a strong sense about him. There was something behind his eyes that she recognized. The same something that seemed to live within herself.

Is that it? she wondered. *Is that why things are always so confusing with Noah?* If he was as screwed up as she was, it might explain why she felt drawn to him. Of course, it would also explain why they were doomed.

The best thing would be to forget about both Noah and Burke. Since when did she need to have a guy in her life? She'd never had one before. Trusting people with her feelings now would only get her hurt—and maybe hurt other people as well.

After all, she might not ever make the train home.

At that moment, a male voice with a thick Scottish brogue came over the loudspeaker. "We are approaching Edinburgh. Please make sure to claim your belongings."

As the train came to a loud, squeaky halt, passengers began moving about the car, shouldering bags and lining up along the center aisle. Sydney sat patiently, waiting until most of the people cleared out. Then she picked up her bag and headed out into the station.

She mounted a set of cement steps to the street level and gazed about the city. An early-evening rain had darkened the tall brick buildings and left the cobblestone roads wet and polished-looking. On the hill to her right loomed Edinburgh Castle, like the backdrop of a movie.

Sydney strode briskly down the sidewalk, passing a long line of shops hawking wools, tartans, cashmere sweaters, and cheesy plastic souvenirs. A man in a green kilt stood outside a hotel lobby, helping wealthy-looking tourists from their cabs. The high, reedy notes of a bagpipe wafted from a nearby pub.

The pubs with quaint wooden signs, the people with Scottish accents, and the light mist gave her a heady feeling. *I'm really here. In Scotland.* She wished she could bring back a kilt for Francie. *She'd get a kick out of that.*

As she walked along, Sydney could feel herself sliding into fifth gear. Her senses sharpened, her body became alert, and her mind bundled up all extraneous thoughts and concerns, leaving her free to focus on the task at hand—namely, finding the SD-6 safehouse and her European contacts.

Wilson's directions led her down North Bridge to High Street and then to a maze of back alleys. She turned into the second one she came to. A row of weathered wooden doors checkered the back walls of the buildings. Sydney approached the third door on the left and rapped on it loudly. Three quick knocks, followed by three slower ones.

Almost immediately the door opened and a round-faced man with a bushy black mustache poked his head out. He ushered her inside while quickly glancing to and fro, and bolted the door behind her. Inside, it was pitch-black.

"Follow me," the man said gruffly, switching on a flashlight.

He led her up two flights of stairs to a small landing. Doors stood to the right and left, and a weak beam of sunlight shone through a high transom window. The door on the left was wide open. Peeking through it, Sydney could see a dusty room containing a few abandoned power tools and two rickety sawhorses holding up planks of plywood.

The door to the right was shut tight. The man walked over and slowly pushed it open, beckoning her to follow. Inside was a small, cramped space with dozens of cardboard boxes piled high in towers, a few even reaching the ceiling. There was barely any room to walk. Sydney was just beginning to wonder why he'd led her in there when the man hit a hidden switch. Instantly, a side wall slid open, revealing a narrow passageway.

They ducked through the opening into a wide, windowless space, this one full of computers and radio equipment. A husky blond man was sitting at one of the monitors. As soon as they entered, he took off his headphones and stood up.

"That's Donaldson," said the mustached man, gesturing toward the blond guy. "And I'm Pinelli."

"You're a little young, aren't you?" Donaldson said. He was American. "How old *are* you?"

"Old enough," she replied.

Donaldson shook his head. "I don't like this, Pinelli. Look at her. She can't be more than twenty. What kind of a—?"

"Save it." Pinelli held up a stubby hand. "You want to complain to the boss, go ahead. But I'm not covering your ass. Besides, I saw her file. She's got the right stuff."

Sydney stood unwavering while Donaldson fixed her with a long, hard stare. Eventually he sank back into his chair. "It's your call, P. But I'm not here to do any baby-sitting." He swiveled toward the monitor and jammed the headphones back onto his head.

Pinelli placed his fingers on her arm and guided her to the other side of the room. "Don't mind him. He's a hothead, but he's a good agent. He's just a little thrown because you're so . . ."

"Young?" Sydney concluded irritably.

Pinelli nodded. "And female and pretty. He's under the impression that only big, ugly lunkheads like him can do the business."

"I know the type," Sydney muttered.

"But I don't have any doubts," Pinelli went on. "Wilson and I go way back. He trained me. And I've never heard him express such a high opinion about anyone the way he did for you. If he says you're the one for the job, then you are."

Sydney tried to stay plain-faced and professional, but her mouth automatically curved upward. It felt good to know Wilson had praised her.

"All right," Pinelli said, glancing at his watch. "We've got a little more than five hours until drop-off time. I'll go over the itinerary and check supplies; Donaldson will check the latest satellites and infrareds."

"What about me?" she asked.

"Get changed. We've got wigs, makeup, and wardrobe in that room through there."

She followed his finger to a smaller, adjoining room in the far corner.

"Grab what you need, and take as long as you want," he went on. "Just make sure when you come out you're no longer Agent Bristow . . . but Adriana Nichita."

7

THE LOCH NESS MONSTER.

Ever since they'd begun their journey west in their boxy black van, it was all Sydney could think about. Looking out the tinted windows, she glimpsed the hard, almost mystical-looking terrain. As they bumped along the left side of a rough two-lane highway, the surrounding countryside varied from grassy pastures to windswept heaths to rocky lunar landscapes. A few times they passed the crumbling remains of a castle or an old fortress. And tucked here and there between the heather-covered hills were long, narrow chasms filled with midnight blue water. The lochs.

Without intending to, without even being a believer, she found herself trying to catch a glimpse of the famous tapered head and bowed, slender neck.

Sydney was completely entranced by the wild beauty of western Scotland. There was a scrappy hardiness about it. The same deep-seated stoutness that had been bred within herself.

"We're only a few minutes out now," Pinelli said, twisting around in the left front passenger seat to face her. "You might want to do a final check."

"Right. Thanks."

Sydney ran a hand over her head. Her hair had been squeezed inside a mesh cap so tight, she could almost feel it reshaping her skull. On top of that, she'd fitted a snug wig, mirroring the sleek black, bobbed hairstyle from Adriana's file photo. A pair of special contact lenses floated over her irises, changing them from deep chestnut to Adriana's lighter, amber-like hue.

Wilson had seen to everything. Her black pantsuit and boots had European labels. Her diamond stud earrings and white platinum Rolex glittered. Her leather Louis Vuitton luggage was filled with appropriate changes of clothing, and a coordinating Prada handbag was crammed full of both British and Italian currencies, since an Italian island was one of Adriana's last known whereabouts before her arrest. The bag even held an antique gold compact mirror with the letter *N* etched on the top.

Sydney removed the compact, powdered her nose and cheeks, and applied one more coating of wine-colored lipstick. Then she carefully studied her face in the small round mirror. She didn't look like herself at all. She didn't even feel like herself. Her chin was raised at a higher, more privileged angle, and her newly manicured nails made her hand gestures more elegant and sweeping.

She was Adriana Nichita. Pampered yet sheltered, and bitter about losing the life of power she'd been born to inherit.

"You all set?" Pinelli asked.

"I'm ready," she replied, her voice taking on the lilting cadence of a native Romanian.

Pinelli grinned. "Good." He gestured toward Donaldson, who sat on the right, sullenly driving the van. "Remember, we're your bodyguards. Your hired help. Snipe at us and boss us around a bit while we're there."

Sydney brightened at the thought. Maybe she could order Donaldson to lick her boots shiny, or throw himself across a puddle so she could walk over his back.

"Do we have a boat?"

Pinelli nodded. "Fishing boat. There's no regular transportation to Balfour unless you count von Muller's yacht. But in accordance with the rules of the summit, von Muller sent his boat and crew to Aberdeen. Plus, the crossing can be tricky with all the Atlantic currents converging. We felt it better to hire a local than try to pilot a boat ourselves and take unnecessary risks."

"Right." She nodded solemnly.

"After we get there and search the house and grounds, Donaldson and I will head to an outpost where we can visually monitor the island and try to pick up radio signals from the other guests' backup people," Pinelli went on. "A few days ago Donaldson planted the signal device on the lighthouse glass. Check the beam as often as you can. If we have any pertinent information to pass on to you, we'll send it via Morse code. Otherwise, you're on your own." His features wrinkled into a sympathetic gaze.

"I understand." She smiled at him, grateful for his kindness.

"Here's the bay," Donaldson called out, swerving the van into a gravel lot fenced off by wooden poles. Up ahead lay the jagged, rocky coastline and a ramshackle dock. A decrepit forty-foot fishing boat was moored at the far end.

Pinelli jumped out of the van, opened Sydney's door, and offered her a hand. While he checked the latest weather image on a hand-held computer, she slipped into her fur coat and matching muff. Meanwhile,

Donaldson jogged up the pier to check with the boat captain.

A few minutes later Donaldson came puffing back. "The old guy says to get a move on. Bad weather is coming and he needs time to check his traps before the end of the day."

Pinelli and Donaldson grabbed Sydney's luggage out of the back of the van and the three of them headed for the dock, Pinelli offering Sydney his arm to guide her over the rocky path. Once they stepped onto the creaky planks of the pier, Sydney gazed out over the water, searching for the isle. But all she could see were wooly clouds resting along the horizon.

A man stood waiting for them at the end of the dock. His gray hair stuck out in thick bristles beneath his brown knit cap, and his face looked as dry and withered as the parched wooden sides of the boat bobbing in front of them. "Come aboard," he said in a thick brogue. "And mind ye the longlines," he added, pointing to coils of fishing line heaped on the boat floor. "Ye'd hate to go over with a six-inch hook in yer shank."

They stepped onto the swaying boat, Pinelli holding her hand and guiding her like a good manservant. Then he and Donaldson heaped her luggage in a corner while she perched on a narrow, padded bench.

"An' here we go," the captain said, turning the key

and firing the motor. They untied the boat and shoved off.

Sydney felt a lurching sensation inside her. *This is it,* she thought, taking a deep breath of salty sea air. She was now officially embarking on her mission. She'd expected to be filled with dread at this point, but she wasn't. Instead, her mind felt revived, primed with a heavy sense of duty.

She was ready for anything. Even a fabled monster.

* * *

Sydney stood against the rail, gazing out over the choppy waves. The entire world was gray—from the steely water below to the smoky rain clouds above. Soon after they'd left the shore, a gauzy mist appeared all around them, narrowing their view and trapping them in a sullen nothingness. If it weren't for the rhythmic pounding of the surf against their vessel, she would have doubted they were moving at all.

The old boat captain, however, seemed used to such conditions. He half hummed, half whistled a sad-sounding folk tune as he steered the creaky ship through the water.

Sydney walked up beside him. "Is it much farther?" she asked in her newly acquired Romanian accent.

"Not far," he replied, keeping his eyes straight

ahead. "I don't know why ye'll be wanting to see Balfour. 'Tis a small, desolate place. Nothing there but the auld house, and many in these parts swear it's haunted. Many eerie goin's-on and bogeys have been spotted there. Most people think it isn't worth the long crossing, but ye're the third group o' the day to be ferried over."

"Is that so?" she asked, hoping to glean more information.

"Foreign folk. Tourists, like yerselves. No locals would be wantin' a ride, that's for sure. Of course"—he cracked a near-toothless grin and patted the wad of ten-pound notes poking out of his shirt pocket—"I canna say I mind the spare quid."

Sydney smiled. From over the man's shoulder, she spotted Donaldson beckoning to her. "Excuse me," she said to the old man, and walked unsteadily to the back of the boat. "What?" she asked in a whisper.

"You're getting out of character," Donaldson mumbled. "Don't be so friendly. Adriana is a known snob and would never chat with common strangers."

Sydney narrowed her eyes at him. "Fine. From now on I'll be a raving witch." She strode past him and leaned against the frame of the boat, pretending to stare out at the ghostly haze.

She knew she was being a little unfair. After all, he'd made a good point. But she didn't like being scolded. It made her feel like the naïve, clumsy teenager Noah had made her out to be during the first briefing. She did not need to be reminded of that. And it was way past time for doubt to set in.

"There's the island! There's Balfour." The old man's shout broke through her thoughts. She looked over and saw him gesturing toward the mist off the port bow.

She turned and stared in the direction he'd indicated. A second later, a craggy isle appeared through the fog as if magically conjured. The captain had been right. It did look gloomy. Streaks of red granite rose out of the inky water like a bloody fist clutching a small, boulder-strewn spot of earth. There was no greenery except for a few shriveled thatches of weeds and the scrawny skeleton of a tree. And right in the middle stood a large fortress of a house made from dull gray stones.

She could definitely see why some would think it haunted. The mansion was tall and ominous, at least three stories high, and flanked on either side by spindly towers. A jagged, toothy-looking trim edged the roofline, and pale, yellowish candlelight shone from two tall, mullioned windows over the front archway.

The house looked like something from a classic horror film—dreary and colorless. In fact, the only spots of brightness on the whole isle were a large yellow speedboat docked in a small cove and two round, slate-green awnings that topped the front windows. Everything else was the dingy, faded hue of ashes.

The old captain steered the vessel to a small wooden dock jutting from the one sloping area of the isle, and they disembarked. Sydney recognized von Muller standing at the head of the dock wearing a long black coat with a high, round collar and attached cape. A charcoal-colored derby sat on his head, and his gloved hands held an open umbrella.

As they approached, he tipped back the umbrella, lifting the shadow from his face. His mouth was set at the same downturned angle as his thick mustache, and his small, sharp eyes flitted back and forth, appraising each of them in quick, calculating glances. But as soon as Sydney got within a few steps of him, von Muller smiled at her, lifted his hat, and bowed slightly.

"Ah, Adriana," he greeted. "Thank you for coming to my estate. We have much important business to discuss." He grasped her right hand, lifted it to his mouth, and kissed it.

"I would say it's my pleasure, von Muller," she replied, the twinge of Romanian lingering in her icy English greeting. "But, as you say, we are not here for pleasure."

Beside her, Pinelli snorted faintly.

Von Muller's grin weakened slightly. "Yes. Well, won't you come up the path and wait while my men check your belongings? I apologize for this brutish behavior, but I am simply following the rules everyone agreed on."

By now a relentless drizzle was falling and a mass of black clouds was creeping toward the isle. Sydney allowed von Muller to share his umbrella with her as the group made its way up the winding stone path. Once they reached the relative cover of the stone archway, von Muller's henchmen set down Sydney's suitcases, frisked Donaldson and Pinelli, and checked their bag of equipment.

"They're clean," one of them grunted to von Muller.

"Very good." Von Muller gave them a regal nod. "You gentlemen are now free to inspect my home to make certain I too am abiding by the agreement."

Donaldson and Pinelli entered the house with their bag of detection devices, closely followed by one of von Muller's men. The other goon turned toward Sydney, his hands raised to begin frisking. Sydney stepped backward and clutched her coat tightly.

"You will not touch me!" she barked at the man.

The guy looked at von Muller.

"Again, I apologize, Adriana," Von Muller said. "But you must. It is the rule."

Sydney had, of course, known she would need to be frisked, but she couldn't imagine the real Adriana standing for it quite so easily. Fixing von Muller with a glacial stare, she opened her arms and allowed his crony to search her.

"She's clean," the man said once he'd finished.

Sydney made a huffing noise. "I hope you are quite satisfied," she said, lifting her chin. "Now will you welcome me inside? Or must I stay out here in the cold?"

Von Muller held up a gloved hand. "Patience, Adriana. We must still search your luggage."

For the next ten minutes, the henchman rummaged through her suitcases while von Muller stood puffing on a pipe. Sydney tapped the toe of her boot against the stone step, trying to appear miffed as she cased the island, making mental notes of paths and landmarks. She then glanced upward, checking the layout of the roof parapet. She tried to picture herself up there, wearing Graham's harness, desperately waiting for a lift. Hopefully it wouldn't come to that. It would be risky, especially at night. One false move and she could end up falling forward onto the stone steps she was standing on, or backward into the rocky cliffs that rose out of the sea to buttress the rear of the house.

Von Muller's man finished checking her luggage, completely disregarding the special bustier and sunglasses. Just as he was zipping her bags back up, Pinelli, Donaldson, and von Muller's second bodyguard emerged from the mansion.

"Our sweep turned up nothing," Pinelli declared with a shrug.

"What did I tell you?" von Muller said, tapping the bowl of his pipe against the stone wall to empty it. "Now we have all abided by the rules. Our men can leave and we can begin our affairs as respected colleagues." He placed one hand on her elbow and gestured toward the entrance with the other.

"Wait." Sydney stood firm. "You," she said, nodding at Pinelli. She pointed at von Muller. "I want you to frisk him."

Von Muller balked. "What? But my dear, that is not necessary. I have already been frisked by several of the other guests' people."

"That may be so, dear Herbert," Sydney purred mockingly. "But you haven't been frisked by *my* men. Check him well," she ordered Pinelli.

Sydney thought she could detect the barest of smiles on Pinelli as he patted down von Muller and delved into his pockets. The look of narrowly contained fury on von Muller's face made her want to laugh. She'd only done it to teach him a lesson—to one-up him after he'd so thoroughly enjoyed violating her—so she was not quite prepared when Pinelli let out a cry of discovery and held up the umbrella. He unscrewed the long, pointed tip and pulled out a shiny steel pick with a thin, molded handle. The shaft was nearly four inches long and looked razor sharp.

"What's this for?" Pinelli asked, grabbing von Muller and shoving him against the side of the house. Donaldson rushed up and pinned his opposite side. Meanwhile, von Muller's two men loomed menacingly nearby.

"It's a mistake. That's all. An oversight." He looked right at Sydney. "Adriana, I swear. I'd forgotten it was even there. I only pulled it out of my boat because it was raining."

Sydney walked toward him and placed her hands on her hips. "Do you often carry umbrellas with deadly tools hidden inside them, Herbert?"

"I . . . I . . ." His bottom lip spasmed and his pasty complexion became even paler. "You know how it is, Adriana. The way we have to live. You can't be too careful."

Sydney pretended to consider this. She wasn't too surprised that von Muller had stashed a weapon and then lied about it (after all, she herself had sneaked in two prohibited devices), but she wasn't going to let him off that easy. "Very well," she said after letting him squirm a good minute. "But I am afraid you will have to be more careful, Herbert. I will ask my men to take your little toy with them."

"Of course. Yes. Of course," he said as Donaldson

and Pinelli relaxed their grips. The other henchmen backed off, and von Muller stood up straight, pouting as he adjusted his clothes.

"You may leave now, gentlemen," Sydney said, gesturing toward the fishing boat with her fake fingernails.

Donaldson and Pinelli glanced at one another. "You sure you'll be all right, madame?" Pinelli asked, glaring at von Muller.

"Yes. Thank you," she replied. "You will not try anything stupid, will you Herbert?"

"No. Never, my dear. As I said before I only—"

"Fine," she interrupted. "Then let your men go so we can escape this tiresome cold."

Von Muller gave his bodyguards a dismissive wave and they ambled off in the direction of the speedboat.

Donaldson picked up their bag of equipment and headed for the dock. Pinelli lingered for a few seconds, fixing her with an expression that subtly conveyed both caution and encouragement. Then he turned up the collar of his jacket and headed out into the swirling rain behind his partner.

As she watched them go, a dense cloud seemed to close in all around her. She had to admit she was sorry to see them leave—even Donaldson. Her last line of help was disappearing into the mist.

Or maybe not . . . Maybe *she* was the one disappearing.

8

VON MULLER LED HER into a long, wood-paneled foyer. "The others are already here, waiting in the parlor," he said, taking her coat. "I would appreciate it if you would not mention my mistake to the others."

Sydney smiled. "Of course not, Herbert. I realize they may not be quite as understanding as I was."

"Thank you." He bowed his head, removed his hat, coat and gloves, and placed them in a large mahogany wardrobe along with her coat and muff.

They then followed the hall into a large, ornately

furnished sitting area where several people were already gathered. No one was speaking. And no one looked happy to be there.

"Everyone," von Muller called out as he entered the room. "Our last guest has arrived. Adriana Nichita has graced us with her presence."

Sitting on the sofa across from them was a beautiful woman with curly dark hair and oval, cat-like brown eyes. She was wearing a high-collared sleeveless red dress that hugged her figure, ruby earrings, and a glittery jeweled pin in the shape of a butterfly. Her crimson lips were puckered in a pout. She crossed her long, shapely legs.

"Adriana, Carmina Polito. She is here on behalf of Mercado de Sangre," von Muller said, gesturing to the woman.

Carmina gave Sydney a brief up-and-down glance.

A broad-shouldered man on the other end of the couch snuck a peek toward the slit in Carmina's skirt. He was wearing a blazer over a black T-shirt and was handsome, in a dark, savage way. His dense black hair was slicked back over a jutting forehead. His brows were thick, and his nose was shaped like a crooked eagle's beak.

"And this is Konstantin Baranov of K-Directorate," von Muller said. The man in the blazer narrowed his eyes at him before turning his attention back to Carmina.

A small man with a meticulously manicured black beard walked over to Sydney and grasped her hand. "It is so nice to finally meet you, madame," he said in with a heavy Middle Eastern lilt. "I am Asam Rifat of the Red Star. I met your father once before he died. He employed many of my people in his East Berlin operations."

"Of course," she replied. "It is good to find old friends here."

"Don't let Asam fool you. He's nobody's friend," came a thick cockney accent from behind her.

Sydney turned. A tall, slender man with delicate, almost pretty features was leaning against a grandfather clock.

"What would you know about friendship, Hubbard?" Rifat asked, puffing up angrily. "You are nothing but a cheat and a liar."

"And you arms dealers are always so ethical, eh?" The man's pale blue eyes twinkled mischievously. Then he turned and smiled at Sydney. "Nigel Hubbard, at your service."

"Adriana Nichita," she replied.

Nigel's mouth twisted sideways as his gaze traveled up and down her body. "A pleasure," he murmured. "We should definitely get together. We could do a good bit of business, you and I."

Sydney drew her breath, then decided Adriana wouldn't dignify his comment with a reply. Instead, she gave him a withering look and sat down in a nearby parlor chair with her back to him.

"Well now." Von Muller lifted his hands and pivoted to face the assembled crowd. "Since we are all here, why don't I see when tea will be ready?"

He walked over to a rectangular wooden box on the wall next to the grandfather clock and pressed a small black button. A tinny buzzer sounded, traveling through the walls of the house. Within seconds a plump older woman rounded the corner into the room, followed by an equally pudgy boy who looked no older than nine.

"You rang, m'laird?" said the woman, wiping her hands on her apron.

"Yes," von Muller answered. "Adriana, allow me to introduce my hired help for the weekend. This is Mrs. MacDougall and her grandson, Malcolm."

"M'leddy," Mrs. MacDougall greeted her with a tiny curtsying motion. Malcolm ignored her, fixating instead on the pendulum cabinet of the grandfather clock.

"We are all quite famished, Mrs. MacDougall. Will tea be served soon?" von Muller asked.

"Yes, sir. We've just been awaiting the young lass. 'Twill only be a minute. I'll have the boy come fer ye when it's served."

"Very good."

As she turned to head back into the kitchen, she caught sight of Malcolm opening the lower door of the clock. Mrs. MacDougall's smooth, kindly features instantly gathered into a fierce frown.

"Stand offa that!"

Malcolm jumped. "I was jus' lookin', Granny."

"Now what would ye be lookin' inside a coffin clock fer?"

"Fer ghosties. Folks say the house is full o' spirits."

"Deevlick! Hands offa the furniture and hurry yerself into the kitchen afore I give ye a good thrashin'!"

As they left the room, Sydney tried hard to maintain a look of bored contempt. The real Adriana probably wouldn't have found their interchange so amusing.

"Well then," von Muller began, pressing his palms together, "while we wait, we can review the rules. As you know, everyone is confined to the house."

"Pity," Hubbard quipped, shaking his head. "What with the weather so sunny and cheerful-like."

"Also," von Muller continued, raising his voice, "no one is permitted to go down to the cellar or up to the third floor of the house. Access is restricted to the ground floor and the second-floor bedchambers. We have twenty-four hours together before our bodyguards return to take us from the island. During that time, we must focus on our troubles in Suratia. Any other problems we have with one another," he added, glaring from Rifat to Hubbard, "must be put aside for the sake of all."

"And how do we know we can trust each other?" Konstantin asked von Muller. His stare seemed to imply an unspoken challenge.

"Because we are all here, Konstantin," von Muller replied. "We have all of us abided by the no bodyguard, no weapons rules." Sydney noticed he avoided her gaze as he spoke. "And because we have no time for treachery. If we waste our evening on petty quarrels, we will end up losing our hold on Suratia."

"Then we must begin discussions right away," Rifat said, as he continued to pace the floor. Sydney wondered if he'd sat down at all since his arrival. "Prince Xavier could already be dead. Prince Frederique could be chasing out our people this very moment. Let's start now, while we are all together."

Von Muller lifted one of his hands. "Patience, my friend. We will talk after tea."

"But we have too much to consider!" Rifat went on, gesturing wildly with his arms. "Have your servant bring food here and we can eat while we talk! Isn't that better? Adriana, don't you think it wise?"

He turned and looked hopefully at her, his dark, saggy eyes almost pleading. Sydney could tell Rifat thought of her as an ally. But openly aligning herself with him, especially this soon, could be a mistake.

"I am sorry, Asam," she said in a proud yet sympathetic tone. "But I will not eat like an animal. I will have a proper meal in a proper setting."

"Yes. Of course," Rifat said after a moment's pause. "How silly of me to suggest such a thing."

Just then, Malcolm appeared, his round, rosy-cheeked face dotted with crumbs. "Gran says to come fetch yer tea."

"Finally. I'm starved," Hubbard exclaimed, pushing past von Muller and Rifat to follow Malcolm toward the dining room.

"What a vulgar man," Rifat muttered, scowling at Hubbard's back. "Come, Adriana." He held out his arm toward her. "Shall I accompany you?"

Sydney stood and placed her hand on his arm.

"Yes, yes. Come, Carmina," von Muller said, offering his arm. "Ladies should be seated first."

Carmina rose to her feet and shook her long, dark curls off her shoulders. "Stand aside, Herbert," she said in a low, breathy voice. "I am not a child. I shall seat myself."

* * *

Hatred. That's what Sydney sensed. It was almost palpable the way it loomed over them, gathering weight and forcing all the oxygen out of the air.

She had assumed the gathering would be somewhat uncomfortable, but she hadn't counted on it being this volatile. Mealtimes hadn't been all that happy at her own house, but as she sat at the long teakwood table with the others, she felt as if she were attending a highly dysfunctional family reunion.

At the head of the table was von Muller, still glaring at Konstantin, who sat to his right. Next to Konstantin, Carmina perched on her padded, oval-backed chair, staring down at her long scarlet nails. On von Muller's left sat Nigel Hubbard, followed by Sydney and Rifat. She could almost feel the heat brewing between the two obvious adversaries.

"What's taking so long?" Rifat demanded, tugging at his collar. "I thought the boy said all was ready."

"Be still, Asam," von Muller muttered. "It is difficult to serve a meal when all the sharp instruments have been confiscated."

Rifat shook his head. "I don't think your servants are competent."

"They are not my regular servants. We agreed I would hire locals, and the woman and boy passed all the inspections of your security crews."

"Nevertheless, at my estate we have strict consequences for making guests wait unnecessarily. Servants should—"

"Bloody hell, Rifat. If you're such a damn expert, quit bangin' on about it and go show 'em how it's done." Hubbard wagged his thumb in the direction of the kitchen.

Rifat's face resembled a red balloon about to pop. He glared past Sydney at Hubbard, making tiny fishlike motions with his mouth. Then he pushed back his chair and leaped to his feet. "You! You!" he sputtered, pointing at Hubbard. "I refuse to be treated like this!"

Hubbard rolled his eyes. "Set your bum down and quit bellyachin'."

"Von Muller, if you expect me to fully cooperate in this endeavor, I must insist that—"

"Sit, Asam," Konstantin ordered. "Be calm. We are all comrades tonight."

"Are you all on the side of this madman?" Rifat shouted, pointing at Hubbard, who was slouched back in his seat, smirking. "Do you not see how he discredits me? It is not enough that his organization has been systematically stealing business from us, now he must be allowed to humiliate me?"

He stared at each guest one by one, scanning them for traces of loyalty. Von Muller shook his head dismally. Konstantin yawned and stared off into the distance. Carmina rolled her eyes. Eventually his gaze reached Sydney.

"We are all stranded here until tomorrow, Asam. I suggest you make the best of it," she said, weighing her inflections carefully, and fixing her features in what she hoped was a completely neutral expression.

Rifat looked sunken.

"Here we are," Mrs. MacDougall sang out cheerily as she entered the room, pushing an old tea cart. She and Malcolm circled the table, placing steaming bowls and heavily laden plates in front of each guest.

"Eat, Asam," Sydney said, touching his arm with her fingers. "Perhaps things will not feel so dire if you have nourishment."

"No! I do not trust anybody. I do not trust *him*!" He pointed at von Muller. "And I will not risk eating his food!"

"Enough!" von Muller shouted, slapping his palm on the tablecloth. "There is nothing to fear, Asam. Because we did not allow her many cooking tools, Mrs. MacDougall made these pies herself and brought them with her to my house. The soup she made fresh here. My only intention is that you be fed and comfortable for the meeting."

"Then if there is nothing to fear, why not have the boy taste my food?" Rifat gestured toward Malcolm.

Von Muller laughed. "You are being dramatic, Asam."

"If you and your servants truly can be trusted, then they will not mind doing as I ask."

Von Muller stared over at Mrs. MacDougall. She turned and nodded at her grandson. "Go on with ye, lad. Give 'em a wee taste."

"No!"

"Do as I say, boy!"

"No! I don't like mutton pie!"

"Mind yer manners, Malcolm! Taste the good man's broth and pie afore I duff ye!"

Malcolm scrunched up his face and stomped over to Rifat. He picked up the spoon and slurped down a mouthful. Then he grabbed the fork and held it poised over the large helping of pie. He paused for a moment, his features contorting into several fierce expressions for Rifat. Then he scooped out a tiny morsel and popped it in his mouth.

"There!" von Muller exclaimed. "Are you satisfied, Asam?"

Rifat watched the boy chew and swallow before

relaxing back into his seat. "I am contented. But I must make one more demand." He reached into his breast pocket and pulled out a foil package. "It is coffee, from my country. I ask that your servants make it for me and no one else. It is all I will drink while I stay here."

"Very well, sir," Mrs. MacDougall replied. She trotted over and took the parcel from Rifat. She then gave him a fresh spoon and fork. Meanwhile Malcolm trudged poutily back to the kitchen.

"Good," von Muller said, gesturing ceremoniously about the table. "Now we can all have a pleasant meal."

For the next several minutes the party ate in relative silence. Mrs. MacDougall bustled about the table, filling everyone's wineglasses and pouring Rifat a cup of his special brew. The bleak mood of the gathering had become even heavier after Rifat's outbursts. But the housekeeper hummed as she went along, seemingly oblivious to the labored pace of the meal and the sneers volleyed between guests.

Sydney tried to swallow enough food to keep up her energy, but her heightened state of alert seemed to be suppressing her appetite. Having to stay in character while scrutinizing the others was already wearing her down. Eating was a chore in itself. She felt trapped between Hubbard's leering stares and Rifat's sporadic huffing and puffing. Von Muller seemed restless as well. He kept shifting in his chair, tapping his utensils, and sneaking furtive glances toward Carmina and Konstantin.

There was definitely something going on between the K-Directorate and Mercado de Sangre reps. Sydney had noticed strange body movements ever since they sat down at the table. They rarely exchanged looks. In fact, it was almost unnatural what little heed they paid one another. And yet their postures belied a keen, almost rhythmic awareness. When one shifted, the other followed. When one's hand disappeared beneath the table, the other's did as well. Sydney was certain they were passing messages, but she wasn't sure what to do about it.

"Enjoyin' your pie?"

Sydney turned to see Hubbard smiling at her. "I've had better," she replied.

"I bet you have." He leaned in closer. "A tall bird like you ought to have more than that. What's the matter? Afraid of poison like Asam?"

She turned away, focusing instead on the candles flickering in the iron light fixture overhead. "I am not afraid," she said, lifting her chin. "It is difficult to eat properly without the appropriate utensils." She looked back at him and raised an eyebrow. "I do wish I had a sharp knife."

"Bread pudding, m'leddy?"

Sydney glanced up and saw Malcolm standing behind her. The cart was in front of him, now laden with bowls of piping hot pudding.

"No," she replied with a wave of her hand.

"Don't tell me you're watchin' your figure, luv," Hubbard crooned. "Y'know that's my job."

Sydney was just raising her hand to deliver a slap when a yelp of pain rent the air behind her. She spun around and saw Rifat leap to his feet, swiping madly at his lap, where large, steaming mounds of pudding were rolling off his trousers onto the floor.

"The boy!" he sputtered, shaking his fist at Malcolm, who was cowering in the nearby corner. "He did it on purpose! I asked him to take a bite and he dropped the pudding on me!"

Carmina and Konstantin burst out laughing, while Hubbard leaned back his head and guffawed loudly. Mrs. MacDougall stalked over and grabbed Malcolm's upper arm. "Now look what ye did, ye fool lad!" she hollered, shaking him. "Apologize to the good sir!"

"No! 'Twas an accident! I swear!"

"Apologize afore I smack ye!"

"I'm sorry!" he yelled at Rifat, who was still swabbing the top of his pants.

"Good. Now git yer hide in the kitchen and start

the washin'!" Mrs. MacDougall pushed him toward the exit. "Go on now, scoot!"

As Malcolm skulked past her, Sydney noticed his mouth curl up in a subtle sort of glee.

Mrs. MacDougall scowled after him and then turned back to Rifat. "I apologize fer me grandson, sir," she said, her sweet old lady voice returning. "He's got a good heart, but he can be a bit daft at times." She grabbed a fresh linen cloth and bent over to help him.

"Get away from me!" Rifat shouted. Mrs. MacDougall slunk back in fear.

"Cheer up, Rifat," Hubbard quipped. "This could be the only time you have a hot thing in your lap."

Carmina and Konstantin burst out laughing. Even von Muller looked amused. Sydney pretended to go along with the others and gave a ladylike titter into her hand.

"Stop!" Rifat bellowed. "I will not be treated this way!" He turned and shook his fist at Hubbard. "I could kill you! I could kill you all!" he roared. Then he threw down his napkin and stomped out of the room.

Hubbard shook his head. "Poor Rifat. It's a shame his bodyguards didn't consider bread pudding a weapon."

9

AFTER TEA THE GROUP drifted into a large, wood-paneled library to begin the official discussions. The room was large and drafty, its ceiling so high, it was cloaked in darkness. Only a minimal light and warmth radiated from the freshly built fire in the stone fireplace. Sydney felt small and exposed.

Outside the storm raged on. The light tapping of rain had grown to a melancholy rumble. Occasionally there was a crash of thunder, which rattled the panes of glass in the tall, arched windows. Otherwise, the room was silent, the only other sounds being the crackling of the fire and the steady tread of von Muller's shoes as he paced in front of a long, polished teakwood table.

They were waiting for Carmina, who had excused herself to freshen up. As Sydney sat in a high-backed lounger near the fire, she took the opportunity to review what little information she'd gathered on the others.

Rifat was back, having changed clothes, but he was still sulky. He slumped in a brown leather armchair, glowering repeatedly at the rest of them. Sydney noticed he'd stopped trying to ingratiate himself with her, assuming, perhaps, that she was already in league with the others. He was by far the most fretful and fidgety of the bunch.

Nigel, on the other hand, seemed to be enjoying himself more than anyone. He stood leaning against a large bookcase that ran the length of the back wall, smiling smugly as he flipped through the leather-bound volumes. Sydney didn't know what to think of him, but his incessant ogling was making her uncomfortable. Rifat clearly hated him, and the others simply disregarded him—neither overtly with nor against him.

Von Muller, for one, seemed far more interested in Carmina and Konstantin. Sydney watched him pace, chomping on his pipe and staring at Konstantin out of the corner of his eye. Konstantin seemed very much aware of him, too. He looked casual as he slouched back lazily on the red camelback sofa, but beneath his dark, bushy brows, his eyes flitted continually toward von Muller.

"This is inexcusable," Rifat grumbled. "We are wasting far too much time."

"Enough, Asam," Konstantin muttered. "We are growing weary of your complaints. We waited for you to put on fresh pants. Now you can wait for the lady."

The door opened and Carmina walked into the room. The men's postures immediately lifted. Nigel quit slouching against the shelves, von Muller ceased pacing, and Konstantin rose from the sofa. Carmina appeared to take no notice, and yet Sydney thought her movements looked a little too choreographed as she sashayed to the other end of the sofa and sat down. For someone who worked as a spy, Carmina seemed to command a great deal of attention.

Von Muller clapped his hands together. "Let us now begin. As you know, our position with the Suratian monarchy is in serious jeopardy," he said, assuming an authoritative stance on the other side of the table. "If Prince Frederique assumes the throne, our security within that country—indeed, throughout Europe—will be seriously damaged."

"Yes, yes. We know!" Rifat exclaimed, waving his hands impatiently. "What are we going to do about it?"

"This afternoon, before my bodyguards left with all my communication equipment, I received a final update on the situation. Prince Xavier is alive, but deteriorating. And it appears that Prince Frederique is anticipating trouble. According to my people, he is secluded somewhere in the palace and has been gathering troops. Whatever we decide to do, we must do it quickly."

"The question is not what we do, but how we do it," said Konstantin in a patronizing tone. "It is clear that we must assassinate Frederique."

Von Muller's jaw twitched. "I believe there are five other delegates here who have a right to say what we do. Carmina, my dear. What do you think on this matter?"

Carmina shrugged. "I think we must kill him," she said, almost casually.

Von Muller shook his head. "But it is not that easy."

"It's always easy to kill," she countered, her black eyes glittering in the candlelight.

"The big cheese here has a point," Hubbard said, stepping forward and nodding at von Muller. "If we kill the bloke, we've got to make it look like an accident. Otherwise, the rest of the country will turn against us no matter who takes power. It's got to be a bang-up job. No mistakes."

"Then send my people to do it." Konstantin sneered. "This is not a job for petty thieves like you."

Hubbard grinned wryly. "It ain't a job for bloody mentals, either."

Konstantin shook a fist at Hubbard, shouting a string of Russian curses.

"Stop!" von Muller cried. "We must work together!"

Just then, a rattling noise interrupted the bickering. Mrs. MacDougall trotted in, holding a large silver tray between her hands. "'Here's a pot o' tea an' some tarts," she said, casting a merry smile around the room. "Now then . . . who's up for a steamin' tassie?" She lifted a teapot in one hand and a cup and saucer and the other.

"None for me," von Muller said curtly.

"Thank you, mum." Hubbard stepped farther into the light. "I'll have a spot." He took a cup and retreated to his corner, taking loud, slurping sips.

Von Muller tapped his foot irritably while Mrs. MacDougall flitted about, offering drinks to the rest of the guests. Carmina and Konstantin waved her away and she bustled over to Rifat.

"I told you before, I do not drink tea," he bellowed irritably. "I want coffee."

"Thought ye might, so I brewed a separate pot. There now. There's a fresh cup for ye."

Rifat took the mug from her outstretched hand and stared into the vapors snaking up from the rim. He didn't smile, but his expression became softer, less prickly.

"Would ye like me to take a wee nip of it?" Mrs. MacDougall asked. "Just to ease yer mind?"

"No." Rifat shook his head. He hunched over his cup and grunted something that seemed to pass for gratitude to Mrs. MacDougall.

"Ye're welcome," she said, moving on to Sydney.

"Thank you." Sydney tried to sound nonchalant, but she eagerly snatched the bone china cup, leaned back in her seat, and cradled it beneath her face, letting the steam warm the chilled tip of her nose.

"Would ye be wantin' anything else, sir?" Mrs. MacDougall asked von Muller once she'd finished her round.

"No, no. That is all," he said. "You may leave." He waited until she'd pulled the door shut behind her and then thumped his index finger against the table. "Now. We must decide what to do."

"I believe this man is right," Rifat said, pointing to Konstantin. "We should kill the prince, and we should use our best operatives to do the job. Why do we care what Mr. Hubbard says? Why is he even here? His outfit is only good at dealing weapons and trafficking petty street drugs."

"Good enough job for you, eh, Asam?" Hubbard fired back.

Von Muller ignored them. "Let us hear from another." He turned toward Sydney with a slick smile.

"Adriana, my dear. Please, tell us what your thoughts are."

Sydney felt a tingly rush as everyone turned toward her. She fiddled with one of her earrings, ransacking her mind for the best approach. "I think . . . ," she began, "that if I am to pledge money and trust the future of my family's organization with Mr. Baranov, then I have a right to know how it will be done."

"Hear, hear," chimed in Hubbard.

"I am sorry," Konstantin said, "but I will not share my methods with people in this room."

"Perhaps we do not need to assassinate him ourselves," von Muller proposed. He restarted his pacing, stroking his mustache as he walked. "Perhaps we could fund one of his uncles—one who is most sympathetic to us—to challenge him for the throne?"

"Nah, that would take too much time." Hubbard shook his head emphatically. "And I, for one, don't want to be doing business in the middle of a civil war zone."

"Then what do you propose?" Konstantin asked.

Hubbard emerged from his shadowy corner and stood in front of the table. "Why don't we pull out of Suratia altogether? We could woo another nation into becoming our safe zone of operation in Europe."

"No!" Rifat leaped to his feet. "Don't think I don't know what you are doing. You have been planning this all along! You are already in trouble with Suratia for not paying your fees, so you have nothing to lose."

"You're the one in hot water with Suratia, Asam," Hubbard said, smiling derisively. "It was your men that offed the old biddy in the marketplace."

Sydney didn't know what he was talking about, but Rifat certainly did. "That was an unfortunate accident!" Rifat shouted. "Is this the lie you have been spreading? Of course. Now I know. You have *already* begun courting a new country. And you have been making sure that my people do not gain favor so you can take over our part of the market!"

Hubbard burst out laughing. "You're barking! Bloody mental!"

"Gentlemen, gentlemen." Von Muller raised his hands. "Why don't we take a vote? How many here feel that assassination is our only recourse?"

For a moment, everyone stared at one another. Then Carmina, Konstantin, and Rifat raised their hands.

"And how many feel we must consider other options?" Von Muller raised his hand and looked around.

"Aye," Hubbard assented, lazily throwing his right arm in the air.

Sydney felt all eyes turn toward her. Slowly yet resolutely, she raised her right hand. At least now they'd have to continue their debate, and perhaps reveal more of their secrets.

"Your vote-taking comes to nothing, von Muller," Rifat grumbled. "Now what shall we do?"

"We continue the debate," von Muller replied, looking pleased.

Carmina suddenly rose from her chair. "I am tired of all this childish fighting," she said, tossing her hair back over her shoulder. "I wish to go up to my chamber and rest."

"Yes. Yes, you are quite right, Carmina," von Muller said. "Perhaps we should continue this discussion in the morning?"

"No!" Rifat's entire body shook in anger. "There will be too little time! We must have this settled before our people come for us."

"Er . . . is anyone thinking what I'm thinking?" Hubbard nodded toward the flashing, quivering window. "It's bloody Baltic out there. There's a good chance our teams can't fetch us tomorrow."

Sydney felt a tugging inside her. She hadn't thought of that. What if they were stranded there for days? A whole heap of potential problems suddenly loomed. She'd need new excuses for her professors, and for Francie. She'd be stuck eating cold meat pies with a bunch of sullen, paranoid lunatics. And worst of all, her risk of being exposed as a fraud would become greater—much, much greater.

"The skinny pickpocket is correct." Carmina's

red lips curled disdainfully. "We could be stuck in this wretched place for a long time."

"All the more reason to go to bed," Konstantin said, rising from his seat. "We should continue in the morning. Perhaps after some rest everyone will be thinking more clearly." He scanned the group, narrowing his eyes at von Muller, Hubbard, and, finally, Sydney. She mirrored his stony gaze, but inside, her uneasiness magnified.

"Yes, I agree," Sydney said, getting to her feet. "Let us turn in now, Herbert. We are all of us exhausted." She really was tired, having slept so little since leaving L.A. Plus, she was anxious to get up to her bedchamber and check the lighthouse beam for any messages.

Carmina was the first to charge out the door, followed by von Muller, Hubbard, and Rifat. Konstantin lingered behind while Sydney took her last few sips of tea. His presence unnerved her, but she forced herself to appear unflustered, focusing on the warm, rejuvenating drink.

She stood and drained her cup, set it on the small, cloth-draped table beside her, and turned toward the door.

Konstantin cleared his throat loudly. "I think you do not trust me the way you should, Adriana," he said.

She turned to face him.

"Your family and my country," he went on. "We

have had good times and bad times, have we not? But I assure you, I am the one you should stand with. Not von Muller and that wretched pup Hubbard."

"Is that so, Konstantin?" she murmured, arching her brows suspiciously. "Tell me, why should I have faith in you?"

"My comrades and I, we are professionals. We know how to handle such things. Last week I had the pleasure of torturing and killing a CIA agent who was trying to penetrate our Taiwanese outfit." His eyes glinted and his mouth spread into a toothy grin, giving him a rabid, feral look. "You should have heard him scream. Those Americans. They are always so loud."

Sydney tried to mask her horror as she listened to him cackle. Nausea bubbled in the pit of her stomach and an icy wave spread from the center of her chest. But she somehow forced the bile back down her throat and met his eye, compelling her lips to smile. "Very gratifying work, Konstantin. I have no doubt you are quite good at what you do."

Her answer seemed to please him. "So you will consider my request?"

"I shall reflect on it all night."

"Very good." He nodded at her smugly. "We will talk more tomorrow. *Do svidanja.*"

"Do svidanja."

She watched as he picked up a candle and

walked toward the door, his body casting a distorted, hulking shadow over the room.

Sydney waited a full minute after he left, trying to quell the gnawing sensation in her gut. Then she took a deep breath, picked up one of the lit tapers, and headed for the door.

She had just taken a step into the corridor when she ran right into Mrs. MacDougall.

"Och, ye gave me a start," she said with a chuckle, placing a hand on the bodice of her faded blue housedress. "I've jus' come to fetch the tea things. My, but ye look unwell, m'leddy." She peered closely at Sydney, her peacock blue eyes round with concern. "Perhaps ye should go rest a spell?"

Sydney paused, overwhelmed by the woman's warm, motherly presence. She had a sudden urge to droop against her plump shoulder and hear her croon words of reassurance in her thick, choppy accent.

But she remembered what Donaldson said. She remembered who she was. So she brushed on past and headed into the dark corridor, without returning a word or a smile.

10

SYDNEY FOUND HER LUGGAGE in an open room in the middle of the second-floor corridor. Someone—Mrs. MacDougall, she imagined—had already made a small fire in the fireplace, turned down the covers on the large four-poster bed, and lit the candles in the ornate wrought-iron sconces on the wall. Her clothes had been placed in a large oak wardrobe, and a pitcher of water and a goblet stood on a serving tray atop the bedside table.

All the comforts of the dorm suite, she thought. *Except for the remote-controlled Sony and mini fridge.*

She shut and locked the door behind her, set the

candle on top of a dresser, and glanced about the dim chamber. The room had a heavy, musty smell about it, as if it hadn't been used in years. The sheer bed canopy, which had probably been bright white at one time, was now a dingy, toasted hue, and the scroll-patterned fabric on the walls was puckering at the seams. In fact, the only evidence of recent occupants was a freshly gnawed mouse hole along the wooden baseboard.

Just as in the parlor downstairs, a chill hung in the air, occasionally broken by waves of warmth from the fire. Sydney automatically hugged herself. The storm had worsened considerably. Lightning flashed at intervals, illuminating the gloomy room, and the wind howled through every crack and seam in the old castle. A stuffed chair with a crisp linen slipcover had been turned to face the hearth. *Good old Mrs. MacDougall,* Sydney thought as she settled into it, pulled off her boots, and stretched out her feet to warm.

She felt strung out, almost misshapen with fatigue. It was tiring, being someone else. She took off the wig for a moment and massaged her head. It felt itchy and tight. Then she put the hairpiece back on. Despite the locked door, she still felt uneasy. There would be no going back if someone were to walk in and see her long hair spilling onto her shoulders.

Once her hands and toes felt thawed, she got up and rummaged through her things until she found

Graham's diachronic glasses. Then she walked over to the window and pulled aside the thick velvet drape.

The slender, arched panes clattered inside their mullioned frames as the wind and rain beat incessantly against the house. Between the frequent bursts of lightning and the rhythmic sweep of the lighthouse beacon, Sydney managed to piece together a view. The storm looked brutal—almost wrathful against the tiny isle and its inhabitants. Dark towers of seawater rose and fell in the distance. And peering down the cliff, Sydney could see fierce, white-topped waves battering the jagged boulders far below.

She put on the phony sunglasses and stared at the lighthouse beam. Sure enough, the lenses blocked out all but a tiny pulse. The Morse code transmission. Sydney carefully translated as she watched.

Storm worse. Snatch option out. Y-O-Y-O.

Sydney sighed heavily and took off the glasses. *Y-O-Y-O. . . . You're on your own.*

Even if it didn't exactly contain good news, it was nice to get a message. A sign from her people and her real life. And at least they didn't say they'd picked up on any imminent danger. She might be stranded, but at least she was safe.

Of course, should her luck turn, there would be no helicopter rescue. She wondered if Pinelli and Donaldson were working on an alternate escape plan. But what? How could they possibly penetrate the storm to get to her?

Sydney let go of the curtain and sat down on the edge of the bed. Tight, panicky feelings fluttered in her chest. She hadn't realized how much the snatch pickup plan truly meant to her until that moment. But now, knowing she had no options, no clear method of escape, made her feel as if she were slowly suffocating. The gloominess of the old house seemed to settle into her bones.

"Okay, take it easy," she whispered, trying to reassure herself. If Noah and Wilson couldn't be there, she could at least try to take on their role herself. "The worst thing you can do is panic. Just take deep breaths and think things through."

She was alive. She was safe, for now. Everyone assumed she was Adriana, and no one appeared to want to harm her. If she played her cards right, she could easily get through this in one piece.

All these thoughts wheeled through her mind as she slowly undressed and slipped into an ankle-length white silk nightgown. What she really needed to do was sleep. She could worry more tomorrow after she'd rested.

Sydney had just finished burrowing beneath the pile of quilted blankets when a low rapping sounded at her door. She jumped out of bed, checked her wig, and pulled on her matching robe. She wondered who it could be. Perhaps Mrs. MacDougall, coming to lay a mint on her pillow?

She opened the door to find Nigel Hubbard leaning jauntily against the frame. His blazer was off and the top three buttons of his pale blue shirt were undone, revealing a thin horizontal scar under his left collarbone.

"What do you want?" she asked, slipping back into Adriana's proud voice.

His clear green eyes slowly traveled from her feet back up to her frown. "I was in my room next door and could feel the heat from your fire. I thought maybe I'd come in so we could . . . talk?"

Sydney didn't even try to hide her revulsion. "We just finished talking. Downstairs at the meeting."

"Right." His lips curled in a sideways smile. "But I was thinking we could discuss things further, just the two of us. Maybe . . . get to know each other better?"

Sydney stood glaring at him, wondering what Adriana would do. Would she scream and yell? Would she slap his face like a soap opera queen? Her common sense was being drowned out by her own angry impulses, all of which were encouraging her to break his jaw.

"We seem to have a lot in common, you and I," he went on, undeterred by her silence. "We are probably on the same side. After all, I noticed you voted with me at the meeting."

"Don't flatter yourself," she retorted.

Just then, she caught sight of movement behind him. The door to the bedchamber across the hall was open a tiny crack, and someone was peering through, watching them. In the small shaft of candlelight, Sydney could see a sliver of a face with dark eyes, black hair, and ruby red lips. Carmina.

Sydney remembered her last hellish tangle with a member of Mercado de Sangre, a group infamous for collecting bounty for the severed heads of enemy spies. Of all the guests on the isle, Carmina was the one whose suspicions she least wanted to arouse.

"You know, it's right nippy out here in the hall," Hubbard murmured. "Why not be a luv and share your fire?"

"If you are cold," she said through clenched teeth, "go and put on your coat."

He leaned toward her with a devilish glint in his eye. "You know what they say, eh, doll? *Nu te uita la cojoc, ci te uită la ce e sub cojoc.*"

For a split second, Sydney let go of all mannerisms, completely taken aback by his speaking in Romanian. She translated mentally: One should not look at the coat, but what is under the coat.

Yuck.

"That may be, Mr. Hubbard," she replied with an icy grin. "But as they also say, *Porcu-i tot porc si-n ziua de Pasti.*" No fine cloth can hide a clown.

"Just trying to be neighborly and make you feel at home," he said, cocking an eyebrow at her. "As you can see, I'm quite good at *romance* languages."

Give me a break, Sydney thought.

"You liked that last bit? Wait till you hear this." He took a breath and began muttering in a low, raspy voice. To her horror, she understood none of it. It was Romanian—at least, the consonants and inflections seemed right—but nothing at all sounded familiar.

Sydney could feel her scalp start to sweat in spite of the cold, and a paralyzing numbness raced through her limbs. This was bad. Hubbard was probably speaking some filthy street-talk Romanian as a lame come-on, or some specialized vocabulary she'd never gotten around to studying. Either way, she could end up looking like a fool in front of him and Carmina—and possibly even expose herself as a fraud.

This was what she got for blowing off her studies to go to a party with Francie. If she ever got out of this, she'd be the best, most dutiful agent recruit the CIA had ever seen.

Hubbard ceased his muttering and waited expectantly for her reply.

Don't panic, Bristow, she reminded herself. *Think it through.*

"How dare you come here and harass me!" she shouted. "Do not speak to me in that language again. I am no longer a Romanian citizen, and I do not wish to hear it—especially from you!" She stepped back and slammed the door in his face, then quickly locked it.

She leaned against the wall, catching her breath, as the resulting sound waves echoed through the corridor outside. She really hoped they bought it. It was heavy on the drama queen factor, but it was all she could think of to do at the moment. At least Donaldson would be pleased to hear how snotty she'd been.

What I wouldn't give to be back with him and Pinelli, she thought. *Or Wilson. Or*—she shut her eyes as her body throbbed with the memory of a desperate, hungry kiss—*or Noah.*

She walked over to the bed, threw herself onto the mattress, and curled around one of the pillows. She suddenly felt fearful and small, like a child lost in a department store. With no one working alongside her, she had no idea if she was doing a good job. The whole situation was starting to overwhelm her. The house was gloomy, the people were shifty, and her brain ached from being two people simultaneously. She just wasn't sure she could pull the mission off alone anymore.

But then, she hadn't been *entirely* deserted. She

still had Pinelli's messages—her one ray of hope. In fact, there could be one headed her way that very moment. They could have had a recent breakthrough.

Sydney jumped out of bed, grabbed the sunglasses off of her nightstand, and pulled back the drapes to check the coded message again. But it was the same as before.

Y-O-Y-O. You're on your own.

* * *

Sydney awoke with a start, her heart thumping in her ears. She sat up and looked around her bedchamber, remembering where she was. The thumping sounded again, only this time, it didn't seem to come from her, but from somewhere in the room.

She slid out of bed and peered about her, searching for the cause of the noise. It was cold, and difficult to see. The fire had crumbled into glowing coals, and the single taper in her candleholder flared fitfully, its wax overflowing the small basin below it. Her pulse slowed as a quick search revealed no one near. So what had she heard?

The sounds came again, and Sydney traced them to a point in the ceiling above her bed. Someone else must be awake—and on the third floor, the one von Muller said was off limits.

Her heart filled with a frantic resolve. She put on her robe and snatched the half-melted candle from the dresser. If something was going on, she had to find out what it was. Better that then get caught unprepared, or lie tossing and turning for hours on end.

As quietly as possible, she twisted the small, burnished doorknob as far as it would go and gently pulled open the door. Then she padded out into the hallway and closed the door behind her, turning the knob to avoid a loud snap from the latch.

The corridor was ice cold, and heavy with darkness. All the doors were shut tight, and there was no sign of anyone else stirring on their floor. She stealthily crept forward in her dim circle of light until she reached the end of the hall and the staircase. She passed the steps leading downward and tiptoed across to the other side of the landing. Then she lifted her candle and illuminated the circular path to the third floor.

Again she heard the bumping noise. Sydney's heartbeat accelerated. She blew out the candle, set it on the floor, and slowly made her way up the stairs, letting the smooth wooden banister guide her. Whoever it was, she didn't want them to see her. Not until she'd discovered what was going on.

The murky darkness seemed to close in around her, confining her sight to alien shapes and various shades of black. Her ragged breathing and her heart hammering in her ears combined in a disjointed, irregular rhythm. The only other sounds were an occasional groan as the old house shifted and resettled, and the high, mournful note of the wind blasting through breaks in the stones.

Eventually her feet reached the third-floor landing. She paused and stared into the blackness of the passageway, holding her breath and straining to perceive the slightest sound. A moment passed and she heard it again, this time coupled with movement, a rapid shifting of the shadows at the far end of the corridor. A violent chill swept through Sydney's chest. Something was definitely stirring in the darkness ahead.

She gripped the stair rail tightly and took a slow, shuddery breath. The fear she'd managed to drive from her thoughts still asserted itself physically. Her hands trembled, her pulse echoed through her head like a jackhammer, and her nearly useless eyes darted around the cavernous gloom, searching desperately for something to focus on.

After an immeasurable pause, her mind reasserted itself, commanding her limbs forward. She groped her way along the wall toward the spot where the darkness had rippled. Layers of dust and bits of cobwebs clung to her hands, while drafts of stale air swirled the fabric of her gown about her legs.

A chill seemed to snake up off the castle floor,

traveling through her bare feet into the core of her body. She sensed she was almost at the end of the hallway. The distance seemed right. And her vision had sharpened, her eyes able to use the minimal light more efficiently.

She could see a window in front of her. It was nearly invisible behind layers upon layers of thick drapes, but her eyes could make out the glimmers of lightning that briefly outlined it in brightness.

Clunk! Clunk!

The noise sounded again, and Sydney jumped from the nearness of it. It was coming from behind the curtains.

It's just the wind rattling the shutters, she thought, her shoulders slackening with relief. *Great. All this fuss because of a loose window latch. This spooky old house must really be starting to get to me.*

Oh, well. As long as she was up there, she might as well try to bolt the thing so she could get some sleep. At least her trip upstairs wouldn't be for nothing.

She pushed aside the drapes and reached in for the handle. But instead of a cold metal latch, her fingers closed around a very warm, very human arm.

Sydney jumped back with a gasp. Curtains thrashed in every direction, and a pair of hands flailed about. Then a brilliant bolt of lightning sliced through the air outside, illuminating the owner of the arm.

"Malcolm!" she cried, grasping hold of the wiggling boy.

She could hear him suck in his breath. "H-how do ye know me name?"

Another flash of lightning streaked behind the glass, lighting up both of their faces.

"Ah no. It's one of them visiting folk," he said, looking crestfallen. "I thought ye were a ghost. Ye look like one in yer white dressing gown."

"What are you doing up here?" she asked, resuming Adriana's haughty manner.

"Looking fer ghosts. They like attic floors best."

"Does von Muller know you are up here?"

His silence conveyed his guilt. He swung his bare feet as he sat on the window ledge, causing his heels to bang against the wall. *Clunk, clunk!*

"If you do not want me to tell him of your insolence, you must go back to bed at once. Do you understand?"

"Yes."

"Good. Now off with you. Quickly." He brushed past her and ran down the corridor, the now familiar patter of his footsteps reverberating off the walls.

Sydney slapped a hand to her forehead. She would definitely not include this in the mission report.

She waited until her blood pressure had returned to normal and then stole back down the hallway to the stairs. Just as she stepped onto the second-floor landing, another rush of movement caught her attention. This time it came from downstairs, in the direction of the kitchen. At first she assumed it was Malcolm grabbing a snack before he headed off to bed. But as she reached the edge of the hallway, she caught a glimpse of red on the floor below.

She crept down to the curve in the stairwell and leaned against the railing. Sure enough, as she peered through the gap in the balusters, she could see Carmina, still clad in her scarlet dress. She and Konstantin stood whispering together in the doorway to the dining room, their figures mottled by nearby firelight.

What are they doing? she wondered. Those two had been plotting something ever since their arrival. But what? And could it have anything to do with Konstantin's attempt to win her loyalty?

"No!"

A terrified shout suddenly rang out from a nearby bedchamber. Sydney froze, listening. It had sounded like Hubbard.

"No! Don't!" cried the same voice, quaking with fright. Then a long, terrified scream.

Sydney raced up the stairs and down the corridor until she reached Hubbard's chamber. Rifat stood in the open doorway looking wide-eyed and scared. She looked past him into the room, but no one was there.

"What is going on?" she demanded.

Before he could answer, von Muller ran up, followed by Carmina and Konstantin, looking flushed from their mad dash up the stairs.

"What was that?" von Muller barked, fumbling shakily with the belt of his paisley-print robe. "Who screamed?"

"It sounded like Mr. Hubbard," Sydney replied.

"What are *you* doing here?" von Muller asked Rifat, eyeing him suspiciously.

"I heard the scream," Rifat answered, his voice high and trembly. "I came to see what was wrong."

Von Muller pushed past him into the room. "Mr. Hubbard?" he called out. Sydney entered behind him, followed by Carmina and Konstantin, while Rifat remained on the threshold, stiff with fear.

"There is no one here," Carmina observed, circling the four-poster bed.

"Over here," Konstantin called. He stood in the dark far corner, motioning with his hand. The four of them approached, including Rifat, who'd snapped out of his trance.

On the wall in front of them, a pair of thick drapes billowed in the frigid breeze. Konstantin pulled the drapes aside, and they could see that the tall, double-lancet window was wide open.

"Look here," Konstantin said, pointing down at the floor.

Von Muller grabbed a lit candle off a nearby table and held it forward. On the floor, several fresh drops of blood were being diluted by splatters of rain. Sydney followed the drips up the wall to the mullioned window panels. On the edge of one pane, something small and blue caught her eye. She reached forward and steadied the glass.

"Look at this," she said, pointing to the small piece of blue cloth stuck on the sharp edge of the lead frame. "It is from Hubbard's shirt."

"Then where is Hubbard?" Carmina asked. Almost instantly, a look of horror came over her face. "Do you think . . . ?"

Sydney leaned forward and poked her head out the window. The fierce wind snatched her breath from her, and icy rain pelted her face. As white veins of lightning illuminated the sky, she craned her neck and searched the area below.

But she saw no sign of Hubbard. Just the raging surf colliding with the jagged rocks at the base of the cliff.

11

NOW THE STORM RAGED inside as well as outside. Everyone was shouting, their voices combining into a discordant rumbling that rivaled the wind and thunder.

"Enough!" von Muller shouted through the din. "I wish to get to the bottom of this! Immediately!" He turned toward Sydney. "Adriana. What did you see?"

Sydney took a deep breath. "Nothing," she said, mopping her rain-streaked face with the sleeve of her robe. "I only heard the screaming and yelling and came to investigate."

"And what did you find?"

"I saw him." She pointed at Rifat. "Then you and the others came."

Her answer seemed to please von Muller. "I see," he muttered. He spun toward Rifat. "So you finally saw a chance to eliminate your rival, Asam. We all know you hated him. And now you use my meeting as a chance to seek revenge!"

"It is not true!" Rifat glared at von Muller, his eyes so wide they seemed almost lidless. "You should ask them what happened!" He pointed at Carmina and Konstantin. "I saw them leave their rooms. They were up to something. They could have killed him together!"

Von Muller's face turned the color of skim milk. He turned and stared blankly at Carmina and Konstantin.

"Pendejo!" Carmina snapped at Rifat. "It is not true! We did not kill the stupid man."

"Then what *were* you doing, Carmina?" von Muller asked, his voice oddly quiet.

"You should be asking this one!" Carmina jutted her chin toward Sydney. "I saw them. She and Hubbard. They were at her room, talking."

All eyes fell on Sydney. A prickly feeling spread over her skin, but she held her gaze steady. "Yes, it is true. He came trying to charm his way into my bedroom," she explained. "But I told him to leave and slammed the door. I can get rid of scumbags without killing them."

"What about you, von Muller?" Konstantin asked, lifting a bushy brow. "Where were you when this . . . unfortunate incident took place?"

Von Muller looked affronted. "I was asleep in my chamber!"

Sydney peered at him closely. Something was glistening on his left cheek. "What is that?" she asked, pointing.

"What?" he asked.

She took the candle out of his hand and raised it toward him. "It appears you have blood on your face, Herbert."

Konstantin and Rifat rushed forward, squinting at the tiny curved cut beneath his eye. Von Muller touched a finger to his cheek and stared, dumbfounded, at the red smear on his fingers. "I . . . must have cut myself shaving."

"That is a fresh wound," Rifat observed, narrowing his eyes at von Muller. "What man shaves at this hour of the night?"

Konstantin grabbed von Muller's chin roughly and stared at the wound. "To me it looks more like a scratch than a razor cut. Did you fight with someone tonight, von Muller?" he probed.

Von Muller angrily shoved Konstantin's hand away.

"I knew it! You killed Hubbard!" Rifat shouted. "You have led us all into a trap!"

"I killed no one!" von Muller cried.

There was a sudden pounding of footsteps, and Mrs. MacDougall, clad in a worn, quilted housecoat, appeared in the dim light, followed closely by Malcolm. The boy met Sydney's stare and glanced away guiltily.

"Sir? Sir, is everything all right?" Mrs. MacDougall asked, wringing her hands. "We heard a fearsome commotion."

Von Muller smoothed the front of his robe and pushed past Rifat and Konstantin. "There has been an accident, Mrs. MacDougall," he explained, his tone once again confident and commanding. "It appears that Mr. Hubbard has fallen out of his window."

Mrs. MacDougall cupped her hands around her mouth. "Sweet Mother Mary!" she whispered. "Oh, the poor man!" Malcolm stood on his toes, eagerly trying to peer into Hubbard's room.

"Yes, it is regrettable," von Muller said, shaking his head.

Konstantin snorted disdainfully.

"Perhaps we should all go to the parlor and calm down," von Muller went on, glaring at Konstantin. "Would you fix us a pot of hot tea, Mrs. MacDougall?"

"Yes, sir. Right away," she replied in a shaky voice. She pulled a handkerchief out of a pocket and dabbed her nose. "Poor, poor Mr. Hubbard," she muttered as she headed down the corridor.

"And make me coffee," Rifat called after her.

Mrs. MacDougall paused, turned halfway around, and narrowed her eyes at Rifat. "Yes, sir!" she replied, her voice an angry sizzle. Then she spun back around and waddled off into the murky darkness.

* * *

Sydney sat curled up in a heavy leather armchair, staring at the orange-red flames twisting in the fireplace. She crossed her arms over her chest, rubbing them with her hands. The fire was blazing at full force, but she was still cold. A chill that came from intense suspicion clouded the room like an arctic squall. Von Muller and the rest of the guests were scattered about the parlor, scowling at one another or staring pensively into space. No one had wanted to venture outside to see if Hubbard's body could be located. It was understood by all of them that the authorities would not be notified. Only Malcolm slept, his body slumped against one side of the grandfather clock.

A rattling sound drew near. Sydney looked up and saw Mrs. MacDougall rounding the corner with her tea cart. The woman's typically cheerful features were pinched and pale, and Sydney could draw no warmth from them. She sighed and looked back into the fire.

The one friendly face in the house had lost its merry luster.

As Mrs. MacDougall handed out cups of tea and shoved a coffee mug at Rifat, Sydney reviewed the evening's events.

Hubbard was clearly dead, and not by accident. But who had pushed him out the window? And why? The only ones she was sure hadn't done it were Carmina, Konstantin, and herself. Von Muller certainly looked suspicious with the fresh cut on his face, but what would be his motive? He and Hubbard had been on the same side during the meeting. And while they didn't seem to be close friends, there also hadn't been obvious hatred between them.

Not like Hubbard and Rifat. Sydney stared at the Turk as he sat frowning over his coffee. He'd definitely hated Hubbard. There were clearly financial motives, what with Hubbard's outfit wooing customers away from Rifat's business, and they'd opposed each other during the vote at the meeting. Plus, Rifat had already been standing in Hubbard's doorway by the time she'd made it down the hall.

Sydney bit the nail of her index finger, and the bitter taste of glue and polish filled her mouth. Her aloneness suddenly seemed even more pronounced than before. Her head was clogged with questions, but she had no one to share them with. She was a castaway in a foreign land, with no allies for miles around.

The grandfather clock made a loud, grinding noise and let out two somber bongs. Malcolm sat up straight and rubbed his eyes. "Two o' the clock," he murmured sleepily. "Witches' tea."

"Why are we just sitting here, doing nothing?" Carmina complained.

"What would you have me do?" von Muller asked. "Would you have me go out in the storm and search the ocean for Hubbard?"

"I like that plan," Konstantin muttered.

Von Muller glared at him, for a total of two dozen times since they'd come downstairs.

"We can do nothing for Hubbard now," Rifat said, absently fingering his beard. "Von Muller will simply have to explain to Hubbard's people why there is no one here for them to pick up tomorrow. But as long as we are all assembled," he said as he set his mug on the table and rose to his feet, "we should at least continue our discussions about Prince Frederique."

"Of course you think we should, Asam," von Muller said stonily, standing to face Rifat. "Now that you have eliminated Hubbard, your side will carry the vote."

Rifat took a step toward him, his face contorting with rage. "How dare you accuse me! You are the host! It is your fault if someone is killed. Especially if it is done by your hand!"

"You're the one who spoke of killing at dinner," von Muller pointed out. "And you were the one we found at the scene. Why not admit it? Everyone knows it was you!"

"You lie!" Rifat was seething. Ropelike veins appeared on his neck. "You lied about the cut on your face! You lied about where you were!" He edged forward until he was inches from von Muller. His eyes were wild with fury, and saliva flew from his mouth. "You are an evil man! A devil! You tricked us all! You wanted us all here so you could . . . could . . ." Rifat stopped, a raspy, wheezing noise escaping from his throat. For a second he stood wavering as the fury in his eyes was replaced by fear.

"Asam?" Sydney said, rising from her chair.

Rifat's eyes bulged frightfully. He stared helplessly at Sydney, his mouth opening and shutting, emitting a horrible gurgling sound. He stumbled forward, clutching his chest until his knees gave out. With a final, choking gasp, he collapsed facedown onto the Oriental rug and was silent.

Mrs. MacDougall screamed. Carmina and Konstantin leaped from their seats while Sydney and von Muller rushed toward the struggling Rifat.

"Asam?" Sydney called, shaking his shoulder.

"Is he dead?" Malcolm asked, pushing through the crowd for a better view.

Sydney placed two fingers against the man's neck. She felt no pulse. "Yes," she replied. "I think so."

"Oh, it's horrible!" Mrs. MacDougall cried, turning away.

Konstantin made a slight *tsk-tsk* noise. "This is what happens to people who drink too much coffee," he muttered. "A fatal heart attack at an early age."

Sydney and von Muller rolled Rifat over. His lips and tongue were swollen, and a rivulet of blood ran out of the corner of his mouth. Sydney looked into his wide, glassy eyes and saw that his pupils were the size of pinpricks.

"No," Sydney said. "I do not think he had a heart attack." She snatched his coffee mug off the table and sniffed the contents. Detectable in the coffee was an unmistakable almond-like scent. "In fact, I am quite sure Asam was poisoned."

12

RIFAT'S BODY LAY IN the hallway, covered with a white tablecloth. From her seat in the parlor, Sydney could see the bottoms of his shoes poking out from under the Battenburg lace trim. It seemed improper, almost indecent for him to lie there that way, like some sort of lumpy carpet runner. But at least Konstantin and von Muller had thought to shroud him after they dragged him out of the parlor.

"I promise you, sir," Mrs. MacDougall, said, pacing nervously by the window. "I didn't kill the poor man. I made the coffee just like before. I swear't!"

"Yes, Mrs. MacDougall," von Muller said wearily.

He stood in front of the fire, staring at the flames as if transfixed. "You have already told us that."

A search of the kitchen after Rifat's death had revealed that someone had laced his stash of coffee with a salty-looking substance—possibly cyanide. Anyone could have done it. But Mrs. MacDougall felt particularly guilty at having brewed the fatal beverage.

Sydney absently fingered the ends of her wig and glanced around at the others. Across from her, Carmina sat draped across the gold chaise longue, looking bored, as usual. Konstantin had uncovered the parlor piano and sat picking out a gloomy dirge. Von Muller continued to peer into the fire, solemnly smoking his pipe. And Mrs. MacDougall kept walking back and forth, kneading her hands and occasionally emitting small, puppy-like whines. Meanwhile, Malcolm half-slumbered in a chair next to the fire he was supposed to be tending, oblivious to all the excitement.

She wondered which of them was behind the killings, and why. And, perhaps more importantly, who would be next?

Once again, she peered down the corridor at Rifat's splayed, duck-footed legs. She thought of his shoes, of how only hours before he had carefully slipped them on and tied them. Now the blood no longer circulated through those feet. Or his hands. Or anywhere in him. He would never take them off again.

Sydney had only seen a dead body once before, on her first mission. The sadistic Mercado de Sangre operative Raul Sandoval. She'd killed him in self-defense, electrocuted him with the sparking end of a live power cord. Seeing his inert, steaming body had been just as much a relief as a shock. But this was different. Rifat hadn't been a friend, but he hadn't been a threat, either. Watching him die had filled her with dread.

Shake it off, she told herself, shifting on the velvet seat cushion to block the view of Rifat's body. She had to keep her wits about her, for the sake of the mission—and her own survival. There was nothing she could do for him now. Besides, this was a man who'd made a living selling weapons of mass destruction to her country's enemies. She shouldn't waste too much time grieving for him.

"What are your plans for the summit now, von Muller?" Carmina asked, tossing her hair haughtily.

"Yes. Tell us your brilliant solution to our predicament," said Konstantin, without lifting his gaze from the piano keys.

"I think you should call off this dreadful meeting and send everyone home," Sydney suggested, masking her uneasiness in Adriana's snooty, irritable tones.

Von Muller turned away from the fire and looked at them. "I cannot do that," he mumbled. "I have no way of contacting anyone on the mainland. No equipment. Not even a flare. We can only wait until our parties arrive to retrieve us."

"But that will be hours from now," Sydney objected.

"Nevertheless, it is all we can do." Von Muller traced his mustache with his fingers, looking grim and haggard. "Besides, we still have not accomplished our task. We have not decided what to do about the situation in Suratia. The vote is again tied."

"Then we discuss it now and get it over with," Carmina said with an angry sweep of her hand.

"I agree. Let us take another vote," Konstantin added, shooting Sydney a self-assured smile. She knew he was convinced she'd changed her mind, that she would now throw her support behind assassination.

Von Muller seemed to notice the change in the Russian's demeanor. He narrowed his eyes at Konstantin, then Sydney. "No. It is very late and we are tired," he said. "Perhaps we should all go back to bed and get some sleep so we can continue our strategy session in the morning."

"And how are we supposed to sleep when two people have already been murdered?" Carmina asked.

"Quite right," Sydney exclaimed. "None of us shall feel safe in our bedchambers."

"The murderer would feel quite safe," Konstantin pointed out. "Notice how calm our host is about returning to bed." He fixed von Muller with a cold smile and leaned back against the piano, creating a discordant crash of keys.

Angry breaths ruffled von Muller's mustache as he met Konstantin's stare. His frown twitched and a faint blue line pulsed down the center of his forehead. "Very well, ladies," he said, keeping his eyes on Konstantin. "Why don't we all go upstairs and repack? Mrs. MacDougall can assist us. We can then gather with our belongings in the parlor and spend the rest of the night together."

"Agreed," said Sydney as she rose to her feet and smoothed the folds of her long silk robe. "But I shall need no assistance," she added, regarding Mrs. MacDougall disdainfully. She hoped to discover more news from Pinelli and Donaldson, and knew it wouldn't be possible with Mrs. MacDougall present.

"Send the maid to me," Carmina said huffily. "I have much to carry."

"Fine." Von Muller nodded. "Then we are all in agreement. Are we not, Mr. Baranov?"

"We are," Konstantin said, standing and stretching his arms lazily. "Although I do hope to get some sleep tonight, and it may not be possible with all of us in the parlor. I have been told, von Muller, that you are a horrible snorer."

He turned and strode out of the parlor, laughing contemptuously.

"He's right scary, that one is," came a small voice from behind Sydney. She whirled around and saw Malcolm, sitting upright, his wide eyes staring after Konstantin. "He has the laugh of a devil."

*   *   *

Sydney shut and locked the door to her bedchamber, set down her candle, and immediately snatched her sunglasses off the dresser. Then she hurried to the window and pushed back the drapes.

She was starving for any scrap of information from her team. She'd been on Balfour Isle less than ten hours, and already two people were dead. And the worst part was, she had no idea who killed them. It was clear someone in the house was on a homicidal streak—and she could very well be the next victim.

If only she knew what to do. Her Romanian lessons and hand-to-hand combat skills seemed useless now. What she needed was advice. Or backup. Or a stealth helicopter circling over the roof to rescue her. Any sort of sign that she wasn't as alone as she felt.

Sydney stared out at the light beacon and put on the glasses. The pulse was still there, blinking intermittently. But it was the same message as before. *Hold position. Y-O-Y-O. . . .*

She ripped off the glasses and sank down onto the

edge of the bed, listening to the forlorn wail of the wind. Pinelli and Donaldson's instructions only filled her with more dread. She'd wanted something to do, some plan of action. Instead, they kept telling her to hold position, stay put, wait. . . . Sydney felt as if she were treading water in a vast ocean with no help in sight. She was safe, at least for now—but her hope was failing fast.

Get a grip, she told herself. *Stay alert. If you lose it now, you'll only end up in more danger.*

Sydney sighed and got back on her feet. The bossy voice of her conscience was right. She couldn't waste time and energy feeling sorry for herself. She had to trust her instincts to get through this. *And after all,* she reminded herself, *I've managed to scrape by on my instincts for most of my life.*

She tossed her glasses back into her purse and scanned the contents of her wardrobe for the most comfortable-looking outfit. Eventually she pulled out some beige twill pants, a long white angora sweater, and a pair of red leather boots. She quickly put them on and checked her wig in the small beveled mirror over the dresser. Her disguise was holding, although the contacts were starting to make her eyes feel dry and itchy. She dipped her forefinger in the pitcher of water and held it over her head, letting a few cool drops fall into her eyes. Then she opened her bags and began to repack.

As she hurriedly folded clothes and laid them inside the yawning leather suitcase, she mentally packed up her anxieties, as well, squeezing them into a small, dense parcel that she could stash in a hidden corner of her mind. It was a process she'd perfected over the years. Somewhere deep inside her, she was vaguely aware of a virtual closet crammed full of such parcels, straining to burst open.

Sydney had just zipped up the first suitcase when a muffled yelling reached her ears. She recognized it as Mrs. MacDougall.

"Malcolm! *Malcolm!* Where are ye, lad?"

She rushed out to the corridor just as Carmina emerged from her room. In the flickering light of the candle sconces, they could see Mrs. MacDougall coming toward them. She ran crookedly down the hall, peering into open rooms and shouting in a high, panic-stricken voice.

"Come out here afore I have yer hide! Come out!"

"What is the matter?" Carmina's sharp, angry voice brought the woman to a sudden halt.

"It's me grandson. He's gone a-missin'. He was supposed to wait fer me in the parlor, but he isn't there. And there's no sign of him in the kitchen or the library or anywhere! Oh, it's this wretched house! There're ill spirits about. I can feel it in me bones!"

"Have you tried looking on the third floor?" Sydney asked, remembering his earlier prowling.

Mrs. MacDougall looked at her, aghast. "No, m'leddy. Folk are not allowed there. Ye know that now."

"Of course I do." Sydney worked hard at erasing every bit of sympathy from her tone. "But . . . it is often in a young boy's nature to break rules, is it not?"

"Not me Malcolm," Mrs. MacDougall insisted, shaking her head. "He's a good lad. He'd never disobey his master."

Don't be so sure, Sydney muttered inwardly.

"What is going on?" Von Muller strode down the corridor, frowning at them.

"Apparently the *niño* has disappeared," Carmina replied indifferently.

"Mrs. MacDougall has checked everywhere but the third floor," Sydney added.

Von Muller tugged thoughtfully on his chin for a moment. "Very well," he said finally. "Adriana and Carmina, would you be so kind as to check the downstairs for the boy? I shall inspect the third floor myself. Mrs. MacDougall, please tell Mr. Baranov to interrupt his packing and help you check the second-floor bedchambers."

"This is intolerable. We are guests. Why should we search for an insolent servant?" Carmina rattled on in her Cuban accent.

"Please, m'leddy," Mrs. MacDougall begged, clasping her hands together in front of her. "This house is an evil place. The lad could be hurt! And he's all I have in the world!"

Carmina crossed her arms irritably and turned away, but it seemed to Sydney that her features were slowly softening. "Very well," she snapped. "I will look for him. But I hope he is to be punished once he is found."

"Yes, yes," Mrs. MacDougall said, wiping her eyes. "Thank you, m'leddy."

"We shall meet back here in ten minutes, with or without the boy," von Muller instructed.

Sydney grabbed a candle out of her room, and she and Carmina made their way to the staircase. "Von Muller is an *imbecil*," Carmina muttered to herself as they slowly descended. "My associates will be very unhappy when they hear about this night. His silly, thieving business will have no more protection from us!"

They had almost reached the ground floor when a piercing scream came from the floor above. Sydney and Carmina glanced at each other, startled, and then dashed back up the stairs.

Mrs. MacDougall was standing in the doorway to Konstantin's bed chamber, tugging at her housecoat and whimpering. They raced forward and peered into the room.

Konstantin was lying on his back in a puddle of blood, a fireplace poker stuck deep in his heart.

13

CARMINA PUSHED PAST SYDNEY and Mrs.
MacDougall. She dropped onto her knees, staring at
Konstantin. "Kostya?" she called hoarsely. "Kostya,
mi amor? *¿Mi vida?*" She lifted her hands and let
them hover shakily over his body. Then she reached
out and gingerly touched his cheek. Konstantin's head
flopped lazily to the side, gazing toward Sydney with
lifeless, vacant eyes.

"No!" Carmina crumpled forward and threw her
arms around him. She sobbed facedown, her head between his chin and the poker, her hands slapping his
sides futilely. Then she slowly rose up, threw back her

head, and began screaming. Horrible, despairing cries that Sydney thought would never end.

Sydney heard the pounding of feet. She turned to see von Muller running toward them, his face white with fright.

"What is it?" he asked, glancing around. "Carmina?"

He stopped at the doorway and looked in at Carmina grieving over Konstantin's bloody form. His back stiffened.

"Mina?" he said, his voice lower and gentler than Sydney had ever heard it before.

Carmina stopped her wailing and stared at him. "You!" she growled. Her eyes were blazing, and strands of black hair stuck to her tear-streaked face.

She rose to her feet and went toward him, her dark eyes flashing with rage. "You did this! You! You could not stand it that I loved him! That I didn't love you!"

Von Muller shook his head and stepped backward into the hall, trapped in her gaze. "No," he whispered. "It wasn't me. I swear, Carmina. My darling."

"Do not lie to me!" she shouted. "You always hated him. Hated him because he won my heart when you could not!"

Von Muller shut his eyes and hung his head. "Mina," he said, half choked. "Don't."

Carmina began to circle him slowly. "Yes, I

loved him," she taunted. "*Him!* I loved him with my heart and my body. I made love to him in *your house!* Your own kitchen, *as you slept!*"

"Don't." Von Muller squeezed his eyes shut. "Don't."

A sudden realization swept through Sydney. Carmina and Konstantin. They'd been lovers, not accomplices. Their odd behavior at dinner had probably been a game of footsie instead of secret message-swapping. And their late-night rendezvous in the pantry had simply been a secret tryst.

Von Muller must have known of their relationship. Or sensed it. And that was why he'd openly disliked Konstantin. Because he wanted Carmina for himself.

"You are a fool!" Carmina spat at von Muller, keeping up her measured pacing around him. "You deserved that scratch I gave you. When you came to my door, begging for my love like a little boy!"

He opened his eyes and stared at her, his mouth lifting into a shaky smile. "But you loved me once," he said feebly.

"*¡Idiota!*" Carmina slapped his face. "The only reason I slept with you in the past was to get information for my agency! You were a mission, a chore—not a lover!"

Von Muller's face seemed to crack from all

sides. His brow furrowed and his mouth twisted as if he were in pain. "No," he murmured.

Carmina ceased her prowling and glared at him, tears streaming down her cheeks. "You should *never* mix love and work. Do you not know that?" She turned to Konstantin's body. "It only comes to grief," she added softly.

Thunder crashed nearby and a flash of lightning shot sudden flares of light through the room.

Without warning, Carmina let out a cry of rage and ripped the butterfly-shaped pin off of her dress. Before Sydney realized what was happening, Carmina lunged forward and swiped at von Muller, severing his throat with one of the thin metal wings.

Von Muller clasped his neck. For a few seconds, he stared at Carmina with wide, wounded eyes. Then he stepped forward and reached for her.

Black-red blood trickled from his neck.

As Carmina backed away, Sydney looked wildly around. How to stop the blood? You couldn't put a tourniquet on someone's neck, could you? To her horror, the trickle turned into a stream. Carmina had sliced him deeper than Sydney realized.

Von Muller stumbled toward Carmina, his shirt drenched with blood. Carmina stumbled backward, slicing back and forth with her pin.

An icy sensation spilled through Sydney's chest. "Carmina!" she shouted.

But it was too late. Carmina, her wide, terrified eyes glued to von Muller, was backing directly toward the stair railing. Just as von Muller gave a last, desperate dive for her, she fell backward and flipped over the banister. Sydney heard the sharp popping sound of breaking wood, and Carmina's scream, followed by a dull thud from the floor below.

Von Muller dropped to his knees, grasped at the air that had once held Carmina, and keeled forward. He lay there, motionless, his bloody right hand hanging over the shattered edge of the landing, still reaching for her.

* * *

Everything became eerily silent. Sydney stood frozen for a moment as the reality of what had happened hit her. Blood was everywhere. Splattered on the walls, the ceiling, even her sweater. A dark channel curved across the corridor, leading from the spot where Carmina first slashed von Muller to where his body had eventually collapsed.

Sydney carefully picked her way to the staircase. Then she raced down the steps to where Carmina lay, awkwardly splayed across the antique Persian rug. Her neck had snapped on impact.

As Sydney knelt beside the body, a feeling of deep sadness came over her. Carmina may have been a killer for Mercado de Sangre, but Sydney had seen a human side of her as well.

The firelight from the hearth glinted off something in Carmina's right hand. The butterfly pin. Sydney pried it from her frozen grip. A line of rubies glimmered along the platinum body of the insect, and its wings appeared to be fashioned out of a lightweight, razor-sharp metal. Possibly titanium. With enough force behind it, it could quite possibly slice through bone.

Sydney laid the pin on Carmina's chest, pulled down a drapery panel, and covered her body with it. Then she turned and mounted the stairs, her head reeling.

Had Carmina been right? Had von Muller murdered Konstantin? It was the most logical conclusion, and yet he'd seemed genuinely truthful when he'd denied it to Carmina. And if he did kill Konstantin, did that mean he killed Hubbard and Rifat, too? If so, why?

At least it was over now. She was safe. Maybe Pinelli or Wilson could help her piece it together once she got out of there.

As she climbed, strange sounds, like a muffled, high-pitched bleating, echoed down the stairwell. She reached the second floor and found Mrs. MacDougall sitting with her arms around her middle, rocking back and forth and crying.

Sydney was about to rush to the woman's side and comfort her when she stopped herself. The mission might essentially be over, but she was still undercover. And she still wasn't in safe hands. She couldn't reveal her true self yet, even to Mrs. MacDougall.

"It is over," she said in the softest voice she assumed Adriana might be capable of. "Get up. We should go downstairs, away from all this mess."

"Oh! There's a fearsome evil about!" Mrs. MacDougall moaned, her brogue thicker than ever. "Deviltry it is! Ghost-craft! They won't rest till we're all in our graves!"

"Don't be foolish." Sydney reached down and placed her hands on Mrs. MacDougall's plump arms, pulling her to her feet. "Come. We must go downstairs and wait until the afternoon when my people arrive." She was grateful that Malcolm had been spared the sight of this. Now if only they could find him.

They hobbled carefully down the stairs. Mrs. MacDougall was still so agitated, Sydney worried the woman might lapse into a fit and fall. Eventually, they reached the first-floor landing. Mrs. MacDougall cried out as she spied Carmina's shrouded form. Sydney quickly steered her away into the parlor, where she flopped, sobbing, onto the chaise longue.

The worst of the storm seemed over. The thunder and lightning were less frequent and more distant. Sydney unlatched one of the large front windows and pushed open a panel. The air outside was still wet and cold, and a gusty wind shook the awning above her. Even if her team had managed to pick up on any trouble, there was no way a helicopter could make it in this weather. She had to keep on alone—flying solo, as it were.

"We should warm ourselves," Sydney said. She shut the window tightly and tossed some tinder onto the dying fire. Then she clapped the grime off her hands and warmed them in the glow of the hearth. It felt good to keep busy. It silenced her mind and steadied her body. She glanced over at Mrs. MacDougall's hunched, tense form and wondered if the same would work for her. "I think you should make us some tea," she said decisively.

Mrs. MacDougall nodded. She stood and headed for the doorway, then stopped and looked pleadingly back toward Sydney. "Please, m'leddy. I must find Malcolm. And I don't want to be alone. These terrible goin's ons have left me all a-flitter!"

Sydney pretended to be exasperated. "Tea will steady our nerves. Then we'll look for your grandson."

Mrs. MacDougall clamped a hand around Sydney's upper arm as they walked through the shadows toward the kitchen. They passed through the main landing, where Carmina lay at the foot of the stairs. Von Muller's hand still reached down from the darkness above, drops of blood raining down from his forefinger. They then made their way down the corridor to the dining room, where they had to step over Rifat's stiff remains. *The entire house is littered with bodies*, Sydney thought, fighting off a wave of panic.

It's over now, she reminded herself. All they had to do was wait.

Once they passed through the door to the kitchen, Mrs. MacDougall finally let go of Sydney and busied herself, lighting tapers, locating cups, and filling a large copper teakettle with water from a nearby pump. She lit a fire on the iron stove and reached for a small ceramic crock with the word *tea* printed on its side. Just as she was lifting off the lid, a strange noise echoed from the floor below. Sydney jumped. Mrs. MacDougall shrieked and threw up her hands, dropping the earthenware pot. Bags of tea and brittle shards of pottery scattered about the floor.

"It's one o' the spirits! He's comin' fer us!" Mrs. MacDougall backed into a corner, sobbing.

"Nonsense!" Sydney exclaimed, trying to mask her own distress. She was exhausted and anxious, and it was becoming more and more difficult to maintain her accent and stay in character. "It is probably the wind."

The sound came again. Only this time it sounded nothing like wind. It was low and animal-like. A faint yet insistent moaning. She glanced around and eventually traced it to a narrow door at the back corner of the kitchen.

Sydney pointed to it. "What is behind there?"

"'Tis only the stairs to the basement scullery, m'leddy," Mrs. MacDougall replied shakily. "No folk are allowed there. The master said—"

"Your master is no longer with us," Sydney interrupted. "I will go and investigate."

"No! Don't m'leddy!" Mrs. MacDougall grabbed her arm, crying harder. "It's witchery! Ye'll be killt fer sure!"

Sydney shook her off. "Stay here!" she ordered. "If I do not return, go and hide somewhere until the other people arrive."

"No! No!" Mrs. MacDougall yelled, growing more frantic. "I'll not stay here by meself! I'll die of fright!"

"Then come with me. But you must stay silent. Do you understand?" Sydney fixed Mrs. MacDougall with an intense stare.

The woman sniffled and nodded.

Sydney grabbed a candlestick and opened the door. Inside was a narrow set of stairs that disappeared into the darkness below. She descended slowly, Mrs. MacDougall directly behind her. The air was dank and musty, and the moaning grew louder with every step they took. Eventually they reached another door. Sydney turned the knob, but it was locked tight.

"Do you have the key?" she whispered to Mrs. MacDougall.

The servant's face glowed white in the candlelight. She thrust her hand into the folds of her housecoat and pulled out a small iron ring with several keys hanging from it. The steel keys jangled in her shaky grip. Sydney closed her hand over them, silencing the noise, and took the ring from Mrs. MacDougall's grasp.

"Which one?" Sydney asked, opening her palm. Mrs. MacDougall pointed quickly, then screwed up her face and backed away from the door.

Sydney eased the key into the lock, turned it until she heard a faint click, and then flung the door wide open.

The room was bitter cold, dark, and nearly empty. Sydney held out her candlestick and glanced about. A fireplace stove gaped dark and ominous along one wall. Along the other stood a couple of wooden barrels, a few burlap bags, and an old sink basin. The floor was covered with piles of ashes shoveled from the hearth oven, and a large mound of rags and linens had been heaped in the middle of the room. A high, narrow window along the top of the far wall was broken, spilling rain and icy air inside.

Sydney sighed in relief. "See, Mrs. MacDougall," she said, gesturing toward the window. "It was the wind, just as I—"

At that moment, the moaning came again, and the pile of rags on the floor wriggled. Mrs. MacDougall gasped and staggered backward. " 'Tis a demon!" she shrieked.

Sydney ventured forward and nudged the mound with her foot. It thrashed again. She reached down and began pushing aside layers of cloth until she came upon the squirming figure of Malcolm. He lay on his side, his hands and feet bound by twine and a handkerchief stuffed inside his mouth.

"Oh, praise the Laird! Malcolm! It's me, Malcolm!" Mrs. MacDougall rushed forward. "What the devil has happened to ye, lad?"

Sydney gently pulled the handkerchief from his mouth. "Yes. Tell us. Who did this to you?"

Malcolm's lips quivered. "A ghost."

"A ghost?" Sydney repeated. "What do you mean? What ghost?"

"Him." He nodded past her toward the exit.

Sydney whirled around and sucked in her breath. There, looming in the doorway in front of her, stood the ghostly pale figure of Nigel Hubbard.

14

SYDNEY HEARD A THUD as Mrs. MacDougall collapsed in a dead faint beside her. But she didn't turn to look. She couldn't. Her eyes would not leave the unearthly sight of Hubbard leering at her. She shook her head slowly. Was she actually seeing a ghost?

And yet there he was. He was pale gray, except for his eyes and lips, which were dark slits. The sleeve of his shirt was torn, and a ruddy line, like dried blood, stood out on his arm.

"H-Hubbard?" she stammered incredulously.

Before she could react, he sprang forward, grabbing her. They tumbled roughly onto the cellar stairway.

Her candle fell to the dirt floor and went out. The keys were suddenly wrenched from her hand. Sydney scrambled up the stairs. *There's no way he's locking me down here,* she thought as she reached the top. He was just a few feet behind her.

She leaped over Rifat's body and ran into the main corridor. Then she instinctively took the darkest route, disappearing into the shadows of the library.

Sydney could only see the embers of the fire and the hulking shapes of the two chairs in front of it, with a tall metal ashtray stand in between. She grabbed the stand and fled to a corner on the far side of the fireplace, waiting.

Seconds later, Hubbard stepped into the room. "I know you are in here," he called out. His cockney accent was gone, replaced by lighter, French-sounding inflections.

Sydney tightened her grip on the stand, holding it like a baseball bat as she stood in the shadows. She tried desperately to still her rapid breathing, and wondered if he could possibly hear her heartbeat, which echoed deafeningly in her ears.

"You might as well give yourself up," he shouted. "*Whoever* you are."

Her pulse accelerated even more. So he had seen through her disguise. He was on to her. Now she had even more to worry about. Even if she managed to escape this lunatic, she was still exposed. She'd failed her mission.

"Yes, I know you're not Adriana," he went on, as if conversing with her thoughts. "I got to know the real Adriana quite intimately when we were both teenagers."

She could hear his footsteps creaking against the stone floor. It sounded as if he was circling the bookcase by the window. She swallowed hard and held her arms as steady as possible. All she had to do was wait until he got within batting range and let him have it.

"Don't feel too bad," he continued, his voice drawing nearer. "You had me fooled for a while. You were taller, but I figured she could have grown since I last saw her. And you looked young for her age. But I thought, Adriana knows how to take care of herself. I even worried you would recognize me, under my disguise."

Sydney's mind whirled. Sure enough, not only was this man not Hubbard's ghost, he wasn't Hubbard either. He wasn't even English. Who was he? And what did he want?

"I thought, Maybe she knows me, but she doesn't want to reveal our affair. Or maybe she doesn't know me through the disguise." He went on talking to himself. "Then I realized you were not who you said. I began to suspect at dinner. The real Adriana had a fierce hatred of mutton. She wouldn't have taken a single bite of that pie. But I decided to give you one final test, just to be sure."

Sydney could see him now. He was standing right in front of the fireplace, his body outlined in the dim orange glow. He crouched down, grabbed a stick from the tinder box and began poking the coals.

"I went to your room after the meeting and showed you my scar," he continued, tossing kindling into the fireplace. "The real Adriana would have had no doubt who I was at that point. But you said nothing. I then spoke in Romanian, even tossed in a few words I made up, wondering how you would react."

Made-up words? Sydney drooped slightly. How could she be so foolish? He'd been testing her with gibberish and she'd completely revealed herself as a fake.

The coals broke into a line of fresh flames, and his face blazed into view. Sydney slid farther back into the canopy of darkness.

She watched as he reached up onto the mantle and brought down a large candelabra. He held it forward into the fire. When he pulled it back, all four candles were lit. He held the light out at arm's length and slowly turned in a circle, scanning the room. Sydney backed as far as she could into the shadows

As he turned toward the cranny on the other side of the hearth, a faint smile glimmered on his boyish features. He stooped down and lifted up a fireplace poker—identical to the one sticking out of Konstantin's chest.

"And now," he said, placing the candelabra on a table, "it's time for us to talk face to face."

In a flash, he ran toward Sydney, the poker raised high in his hand. It was as if he'd known where she was all along. Sydney was startled by his sudden rush of movement, but she quickly pulled her wits together and lunged forward, swinging the ashtray stand with all her strength.

He parried the blow with the fireplace iron. The harsh vibrations of metal on metal traveled up her arms, rattling her teeth. She fled sideways, keeping her weapon pointed at him. He thrust the pointed end of the poker directly toward her, and she whirled the stand around and deflected it, just in time.

On and on they dueled, circling though the vast room in a ferocious, bloodthirsty dance. The metal rods whistled through the air, clanging violently as they collided. Their eyes locked, and Sydney could see a fierce light in the imposter's eyes.

All of a sudden, he swung a mighty blow that

bent the ashtray stand and sent it clattering off into the shadows. Then he dove forward, pinning her down backward against the long table with the length of the poker pressed against her neck.

"You should stand down, lady," he said, slightly out of breath. "You know how good I am with this tool."

"So it *was* you." She stared back at him in revulsion. "You killed Konstantin."

He nodded. "I did."

"Did you kill Rifat, too?"

"Yes," he replied in a somber voice. "Both very undignified deaths, but then von Muller's rules made it difficult. The poison I had pressed into the tread of my shoes, sneaking it past his guards, and the poker . . . well, the poker was simply handy. Like this one."

He pressed down even harder. The sharp edge of the table dug into Sydney's spine. So this was it. Now he was going to crush her throat and kill her. Yet another undignified death. If she could only buy some more time. Maybe she could just keep him talking?

"But why?" she rasped. "Why did you kill them?"

The imposter glared at her suspiciously. "No! It's your turn to talk. Tell me. Who are you? Who sent you here?"

Sydney glowered back at him. It was unacceptable, failing like this. But if she had to die, she would die loyal to her country.

He reached up with one hand and snatched the wig off of her head. The cap came with it, and Sydney felt her own hair tumble freely onto the tabletop.

"Tell me!" he yelled. "Or I'll relieve you of your real scalp!"

With one of his hands off the poker, she sensed a change in his equilibrium—a slight shifting of pressure onto her right side. Taking the opportunity, she kicked her left knee into his groin. As his body recoiled, she slid her hands under the left side of the poker and pushed it as hard as she could. It flipped sideways and crashed into his head, sending him sprawling to the floor.

Sydney bolted from the room and down the corridor. She needed to hide again—in a better place this time. No! She needed a weapon. A real one. Something like . . . *Carmina's brooch!*

She ran through the parlor toward the first-floor landing. Behind her, she could hear the man's angry grunts and rapid tread. He was coming after her again. She had to be fast. She raced over to Carmina's lifeless form and yanked the window drape off her. In her haste, however, she knocked the pin from its resting place. She heard it skitter along the floor someplace out of sight. Sydney fell to her knees, searching everywhere with her eyes and hands.

Just then, the imposter rounded the corner. He

leaped at Sydney, throwing punch after angry punch. She dodged his jabs, ducked under his arm, and elbowed him in the ribs. As he crumpled forward, something shiny caught her eye. Carmina's pin was lying a few feet away, beneath a dusty antique chest.

She was just about to run toward it when the man grabbed her legs from behind. She fell flat on her stomach, knocking the wind from her lungs and causing her teeth to clamp down on her tongue. The warm, pungent taste of blood filled her mouth.

She kicked and squirmed and managed to roll over onto her back.

"Who are you?" the man shouted as he clawed at her, trying to pin down her arms.

Sydney butted him with her head and he cried out. Blood gushed from his nostrils and his hands instinctively flew to his nose. She scrambled to a sitting position and crawled toward the pin, which was now only a foot away.

She was just about to grasp it when the man's hand grabbed her shoulder and roughly spun her around. "This is the last time I will ask you," he said, holding the pointed end of a candlestick an inch away from her face. *"Who . . . are . . . you?"*

Sydney slumped against the floor as if giving up. She fixed him with a broken, defeated look as her left hand inched beneath the nearby chest.

"I'm . . . ," she began, blood dribbling out of her mouth. He listened intently as he kneeled on her legs, the spiked base of the candlestick still poised above her. "I'm . . ." Just then her hand found the pin. ". . . not telling!" she finished, arching upward suddenly and bucking him onto his back. The candleholder fell from his hand and rolled out of reach.

"Now," she said, pinning him down and dancing a razor-sharp wing in front of his eyes. "Tell me who *you* are."

The man let out his breath and stared back at her with a proud, steely gaze. "I am Frederique," he replied. "Crown Prince of Suratia."

* * *

"You're . . . who?" Sydney felt as if she'd been jerked awake from a dream. She wasn't sure what was real anymore.

"I am Prince Frederique," he said again, a tinge of irritation in his voice.

"But . . . I don't understand." She shook her head slowly, trying to determine if he really was who he said he was. "Why are you here?"

"I heard about the meeting, and I couldn't pass up the opportunity to cripple the forces that have hurt my country for so long," he said. He shook his head and stared thoughtfully into the distance. "I wouldn't feel worthy of my throne unless I'd taken action against these threats. And I knew it wouldn't be fair to risk my people's lives in this matter when it was my family that put them in this predicament. So I decided to come alone. I tracked the real Hubbard down in London and quietly . . . *took care* of him. Then I shaved off my beard and cut and dyed my hair to match his. I arrived here a couple of days later as Hubbard, and I faked his death so I could go about my business in secret."

"But how did you survive the fall?"

"I didn't fall," he replied, looking back at her. "My country is mountainous. Climbing up to the roof parapet was easy for me. The stone tracery made excellent grips."

"How do I know you're telling the truth?"

"You don't," he said. "I couldn't exactly bring a scepter with me."

"And you disguised yourself as a ghost in case any of us spotted you?" Sydney asked. She reached forward and rubbed some gray powder off his forehead.

The prince laughed and shook his head. "Not on purpose," he said. "I needed a place where I could hide. So I climbed down a stone buttress on the other side of the house, kicked open the cellar window, and dove inside. I landed on a pile of ashes shoveled out of the cooking stove. I was quite wet from the storm and they stuck to me like glue. When Malcolm saw me, he assumed I was a ghost."

Sydney frowned at him, studying his features more closely. He no longer resembled a bloodthirsty devil. He looked proud, determined, and very weary. The angry intensity with which he fought her hadn't stemmed from homicidal mania, but from a strong sense of purpose. She believed him. He was Prince Frederique. He'd been on a mission, just like her. A mission to protect his country.

"All right. I am prepared to die now," he said in a tired yet confident voice. "But I ask one thing. I would like to know who you are before you kill me."

His words jolted Sydney from her thoughts. She stared from his eyes to the blade gleaming between her fingers. It occurred to her that *he* thought *she* was evil and corrupt. As they fought, she must have looked just as maniacal to him as he had to her.

She lowered her arm with the weapon and held out her other hand. "My name is Sydney Bristow. And I work for the CIA."

"The CIA?" He smiled and grasped her out-stretched palm, shaking it firmly. "Well then, it's nice to meet you, Ms. Bristow. And I'm glad to hear you'll be keeping me alive, because I think you need my help."

"Your help?" she repeated. She stood and wiped the blood off her face with the sleeve of her sweater.

The prince blotted his own bloody face with the bottom of his shirt. "You have to get off this island," he explained. "If you're the only representative left alive when everyone's entourages arrive, your identity could be revealed, and they'll probably suspect you as the killer." He carefully rose to his feet and fixed her with a sympathetic stare. "I've only planned an escape for one person, but maybe we can manage something together."

Sydney hesitated. She wasn't sure what she should do. Only minutes before she had been in a brutal battle with this guy. Now she was going to place her life in his hands? "I don't know," she said, shaking her head. "I'll probably just figure something out on my own."

Prince Frederique considered her. "I think we're very much the same, you and I. We're used to handling problems alone. But"—his voice became grave— "you have to trust me now. For your safety. And for the sake of your own mission and country."

She looked at him and saw the urgency behind his eyes. *He's right,* she thought mournfully. *I have no other choice.*

Things were pretty bleak if she had to team up with someone who'd been systematically killing people in cold blood. But she couldn't let down

SD-6. And she didn't want to die on that cold, gloomy isle. She wanted to go home.

Besides, the prince didn't seem threatening to her anymore. She didn't want to, but her instincts were telling her to trust him.

"All right. Tell me your escape plan," she said, smiling weakly. "Maybe I'll come up with an idea."

15

SYDNEY WALKED CAREFULLY OVER the sandy soil, her eyes straining against the heavy darkness to make out gaping crevices or boulders. Lighting the path would have been too risky. It would have alerted each representative's camps and caused everyone to converge, en masse, on the isle. At least the storm had abated. There was no more lightning, and the rain was now a swirl of wetness rather than a steady torrent of drops.

Prince Frederique strode softly beside her. After working on their plan for the last two hours, she felt much better about him, admired him even. She still hadn't entirely let go of her caution, but it felt good to have an ally at last.

"Are you sure Mrs. MacDougall and Malcolm will be all right?" she asked as they scrambled over an outcropping of rock.

"Yes," he said with a slight chuckle. "No one will suspect an old woman and boy babbling on about ghosts. Besides, it will be clear that *someone* locked them in the cellar."

"I don't know. I still feel bad," she said. "I just wish I could have been nicer to them." She wondered what they would think when "Adriana's" watch, a shoe, and her blouse tinted with von Muller's blood were found on shore. Would they think she had drowned? Or would they think she had met an untimely end at the hands of "a ghostie"? She'd never know.

Frederique pushed himself upright and held a hand out toward her. "You make a good spy, Sydney," he said, pulling her onto the wide, flat stone. "You played your part very well."

"So did you," she added. "You really had me fooled. What a shock. If I'd known you were the prince . . ." She paused, shaking her head.

He nodded. "I know, I can't believe I had a friend here after all. I felt so alone in my purpose."

Sydney felt a twisting in her gut. "But I didn't come here to kill anyone," she said defensively. "I only came to listen and watch. To find out what they were planning."

"Oh? You never kill while on an assignment?"

She thought of her first mission. "Not if I can help it," she said.

They continued marching downhill, picking their way among the treacherous gaps and loose piles of stones that fringed the edges of the island. As they plodded along, the question that had been needling her ever since he had introduced himself spilled out of her mouth before she could stop it.

"How do you do it?" she asked, struggling to see his face in the darkness. "How can you kill so easily?"

There was a long pause. "It's not easy," the prince replied finally. "But treachery is all these people know. Sometimes killing is your only option. At least von Muller and Carmina spared me some of my work." He sighed heavily, and Sydney thought she could detect a note of sadness in his voice.

"But . . . you're married. Right?" she asked.

"Yes," he answered, sounding confused. She realized how impudent she was being, but she couldn't help herself. She had to know.

"Does your wife know you're here, doing this?"

"No. She thinks I'm in the palace, planning with my advisors."

"But how can you do this to her?" Sydney went

on, too wound up to stop. "How can you risk your life and keep these terrible secret things from her if you love her?"

"It is *because* I love my wife and country that I'm doing this," he replied. "If you don't have love in your life, these things mean nothing."

Sydney walked quietly for a moment, thinking this over.

"I'm not a vicious murderer. I don't kill innocent people," he went on. "I would have never harmed Mrs. MacDougall or Malcolm. Their hands aren't stained like the others'. Malcolm surprised me in the cellar while he was on some sort of ghost hunt, so I had to tie him up. Otherwise, I never would have laid a hand on him. And I didn't want to hurt you before discovering your true identity."

After he disarmed her in the library, he *could* have easily killed her with the poker instead of pinning her against the table. He did seem to have a code of ethics.

By now they had made their way to the rim of the island. A few feet away, at the base of a steep five-foot drop, the surf crashed noisily against the shore. The prince sat, threw his legs over the side, and dropped onto the scrubby beach below. Sydney followed, and he helped to steady her as she landed.

"Good," the prince said, pointing a few yards up the shore. "We're almost there."

"Um, hey." Sydney grabbed his outstretched arm. "I'm sorry about asking you all those things. It was rude of me."

"It's all right," he said. He reached out and grasped the tops of her shoulders. "I am not ashamed of my secret life. It feels good to protect my people. Nor am I ashamed of my role as a husband. After all, if all you have is duty, you are not really alive."

A cold, tingling sensation swept over her, as if she'd suddenly been showered with seawater. She studied the prince's handsome profile in the dim light. His wife and his people must be very lucky to have him.

"Come on," he said as he turned and picked his way the over moss-covered gravel. "We should hurry. It's going to be dawn soon."

They walked along the beach, keeping their backs to the cliffside. Soon they came upon a dense patch of brambles and seaweed.

"It should be somewhere around here," the prince muttered. "Aha!" He reached down and dug through the debris until he'd uncovered a large, dark-colored Jet Ski. "I'm sorry I can't give you a lift, but as you can see"—he patted the back of the craft, where a storage compartment and extra-large engine had been retrofitted behind the small seat—"there is no room."

"How did you get it here?" Sydney asked, helping him pull it out of the mess.

"For the right amount of money, the old fishing captain was happy to hide it here when he circled the island, checking his traps," he explained, yanking long threads of seaweed out of the machine's crevices. "And I told him there'd be an extra fifty quid in it if he kept his mouth shut," he added in Hubbard's Cockney accent.

Sydney laughed.

A minute later, the Jet Ski had been completely cleaned off. The prince stood up and began digging through the storage compartment.

"Here," he said, tossing her a black wet suit. "You'll need this more than I will."

"But—" she began to protest.

"Put in on! Don't argue," he ordered. "Time is short."

Sydney stepped back into the shadows and quickly donned the wet suit. Over it she placed Graham's special harness, with the extra rigging she'd attached to the back. Checking to make sure nothing was loose or twisted, she returned to the spot behind the Jet Ski. The prince then handed her a couple of sturdy, crookedly fashioned hooks that she clipped to the front of her harness.

"Are you ready?" the prince asked, grasping the Jet Ski's handlebars.

She double-checked her clasps and nodded. "I'm ready," she said. "Oh, and . . . thanks. For all your help."

"Don't mention it," he replied. "As they say in Adriana's country, *Nu este bine să fie omul singur.*"

Sydney grinned. It is not good that the man should be alone, she translated. "Quite right, Your Highness," she said. *"Nimic alt mai bun pe lume decât un prieten bun."* No physician like a true friend. "Good luck to you."

"And to you."

He pushed the Jet Ski out into the water and straddled it while Sydney stood at the edge of the waves. The engine purred to life, and he slowly accelerated out to sea.

Sydney took a deep breath and waited. The tow line they'd fashioned from wiring leading to the servants' call box uncoiled, gradually at first, then faster as the Jet Ski increased speed. A few seconds later, the line went taut. There came a violent jolt and Sydney flew forward, her feet skimming the waves.

"Come on, come on," she urged.

Then suddenly, the sail she'd made out of one of the window awnings opened wide in the wind current and lifted her into the air. Her feet left the water and the ocean floor dropped away in a dizzy rush.

Sydney sucked in a deep, rain-soaked breath. *It's working!* she thought excitedly. *The straps are holding!*

Cold wind rushed over her body, pulling back her hair and causing thin tears to seep from the corners of her eyes. She looked down at the herky-jerky world far below. In the velvety predawn light, she could just make out the prince's hunched form and the V-shaped wake of the Jet Ski slicing through the sea. Looking up, she saw breaks in the storm clouds, like the frayed edges of a gray wool blanket. A few tiny stars were peeking through, bouncing their light off the waves.

A faint lavender gleam appeared above the horizon, and Sydney glimpsed the curved line of the coast up ahead. It was almost time.

She could barely hear the prince's whistled signal. She looked down and saw him reach back and sever the tow line with Carmina's pin.

As the line loosened its pull on her body, her makeshift parasail righted itself vertically, pulling her a few feet higher. Sydney had never felt such peace. She raised her arms out to the sides and glided effortlessly in the wind, enjoying the freedom of near weightlessness, high speed, and infinite space.

Look, Daddy, she thought, closing her eyes. *I made a good plane. . . .*

Sydney heard yet another whistle far below her. She looked down and saw the prince waving his arm in a final goodbye. Then he turned his Jet Ski, steering it toward his meeting point farther up the beach. She waved back at him and watched as he faded into the distance.

The coast was closer now. As the night gradually retreated, she could make out the shapes of hills and the narrow stripe of a road. Her momentum had slowed considerably, and she began to sink slowly toward the ocean. She tightened her grasp on her harness straps and prepared herself for entry.

Her drop accelerated quickly. She took a deep breath just as her feet hit the water. A split second later, she was submerged in a cold, wet darkness. Sydney kicked up with all her might, fighting inertia. As soon as she resurfaced, she unbuckled and shed her harness. She swam laterally for several yards until she felt sure she was out of danger of becoming tangled in the lines. Then she pointed herself toward the shore.

For what seemed like an eternity she swam in the icy, gritty water. The whole time, she refused to look toward land, afraid of panicking at the distance. Finally, just as she'd begun to wonder how long her body could withstand the ocean's numbing cold, Sydney's hand brushed against the silty bottom. She felt a rush of excitement. She continued for a few more strokes and then glanced up. Several feet ahead, foamy waves lapped beckoningly against a rocky stretch of beach. She waded to shore and collapsed, her mind almost detachedly noting the first light of morning.

* * *

A hot-fudge sundae? With extra whipped cream?

Pizza with all the toppings, and a side of ranch dressing for the crusts?

Or maybe . . . nachos with spicy chili on top?

Sydney trudged through the misty moorland looking for signs of civilization, fantasizing about what she'd eat when she arrived back home.

She'd been following the beachside road for a while now, but keeping a safe distance in case any enemy agents had tracked her. An early-morning fog helped to shroud her from view. The curls of vapor rising from the ground surrounded her completely, but they also restricted her sight.

She yawned loudly and glanced about, trying to get her bearings. She was just coming around a small heather-clad hillside where the road took a sharp bend and disappeared. As she plodded forward, following the curve, a small, square building suddenly appeared on the other side of the road. In the distance lay a cluster of houses and shops.

Finally! Sydney ran to the nearby structure. She peered through the shuttered windows, but no lights were on inside. The front door was locked too. A carved wooden sign hanging over it read THE GOOSE & FIRKIN in black and gold letters.

It's probably the village pub, she decided, *closed for the morning hangover hours.*

Oh, well. They probably didn't count on any half-drowned American spies stopping by.

As she headed back toward the road, she saw a tall glass phone booth standing at the edge of the pub's parking lot.

Sydney sighed in relief and practically skipped up to the cubicle. It wouldn't be long now. All she had to do was contact SD-6.

She lifted the receiver and punched in her special calling-card code, then entered the number of Pinelli's cell phone.

He answered on the first ring. "Pinelli," he said abruptly. She couldn't believe how close he sounded.

"Hi . . . ," she began, suddenly feeling awkward. "It's me. Sydney."

"Bristow?" His thunderous reply rattled the black plastic receiver. "How . . . ? Where *are* you?"

"It's a long story. But I'm okay. I'm back on the mainland somewhere and I need a ride."

"Hang on!" he said frantically. "I'll have Donaldson trace the call."

Sydney waited patiently, listening to a series of faint clicks and buzzes.

"Still there?" Pinelli came back on line.

"Yep."

"Good. We got the coordinates." A muffled mumbling came over the line. "Just a second. Donaldson wants to say something."

Oh joy, she thought.

"Bristow?" Donaldson's gruff tones sounded in her ear.

"Yes?"

"How did it go?"

"Everything's fine. Except that I'm freezing."

"Okay, listen. We've tracked your position. It's going to take us about thirty minutes to reach you. So stay put, but stay low. Will that be a problem?"

"No."

"Good. We're on our way."

"All right. Bye." Sydney turned the receiver toward its base.

"Wait!" Donaldson yelled.

She paused and lifted it to her ear again. "Yeah?"

"I just wanted to say . . . good job."

Sydney's eyes widened. "Thanks," she said. "Thanks a lot."

She hung up the phone and drummed her nails against the glass side of the booth, smiling to herself.

For some reason, she had an overwhelming urge to call her father. She wanted so badly to hear a familiar voice from back home. More than that, she wanted to tell him all about the mission and share her success with him, just to hear his reaction. Would he listen to her? Would he be proud of her? Would he realize all that he was missing out on be staying so distant?

Sydney sighed and leaned against the booth. Of course, she knew she couldn't really call her father. But it would be nice to talk to someone. . . .

She whirled around, redialed her code, and punched in a new set of numbers.

"This is Wilson. Please leave a message after the beep."

Sydney felt a stab of disappointment. "Hi. It's Sydney. I just wanted to . . . let you know I'm okay. I'll be back soon." She replaced the receiver and shook her head. She really hoped she didn't sound as geeky as she thought she did.

She stepped out into the breeze and looked around. The mist was dissipating, and the full spectrum of colors was seeping into the surrounding landscape.

Her thoughts turned to Prince Frederique. She wondered if he had made it safely to his meeting point. Somehow, she was sure he had. He was probably busy dialing up all his friends and family and his devoted wife, getting comfort from their familiar voices.

She felt the familiar pangs of loneliness. What was it he had said? If someone's life is all about duty, then they aren't really alive?

In a flash she was back in the booth, punching out yet another memorized string of digits.

"Hello?" came a sleepy reply.

Sydney winced. Time difference. Right. She really had to get that down one of these days.

"Hey, Burke. It's Sydney. Sorry to call so late."

"That's okay." His voice became louder, more energetic. "What's up?"

"I was thinking . . . ," she began, absently plucking the telephone cord. "I'll probably be needing some ice cream really soon. Think you could help?"